I0717555

His Majesty's Hounds– Book 2

Sweet and Clean Regency Romance

Intriguing the Viscount

Arietta Richmond

Dreamstone Publishing © 2017

www.dreamstonepublishing.com

ISBN: 1925499170

ISBN-13: 978-1-925499-17-9

Books by Arietta Richmond

His Majesty's Hounds

Claiming the Heart of a Duke

Intriguing the Viscount

Giving a Heart of Lace (a prequel to Winning the Merchant Earl)

Being Lady Harriet's Hero

Enchanting the Duke (coming soon)

Redeeming the Marquess (coming soon)

Healing Lord Barton (coming soon)

Winning the Merchant Earl (coming soon)

Loving the Bitter Baron (coming soon)

Rescuing the Countess (coming soon)

Attracting the Spymaster (coming soon)

The Derbyshire Set

A Gift of Love (Prequel short story)

A Devil's Bargain (Prequel short story - coming soon)

The Earl's Unexpected Bride

The Captain's Compromised Heiress

The Viscount's Unsuitable Affair

The Count's Impetuous Seduction

The Rake's Unlikely Redemption

The Marquess' Scandalous Mistress

A Remembered Face (Bonus short story – coming soon)

The Marchioness' Second Chance (coming soon)

A Viscount's Reluctant Passion (coming soon)

Lady Theodora's Christmas Wish

The Duke's Improper Love (coming soon)

Other Books

The Scottish Governess (coming soon)

The Earl's Reluctant Fiancée (coming soon)

The Crew of the Seadragon's Soul Series, (coming soon - a set of 10 linked novels)

ARIETTA RICHMOND

For everyone who had the grace to be patient while this book, and every other book that I have written, were coming into existence, who provided cups of tea, and food, when the writing would not let me go, and endured countless times being asked for opinions.

For the readers who are coming to know these characters, in this new series, well, as they have come to know the characters in my other series well, and who inspire me to continue, by buying my books!

For my growing team of beta readers and advance reviewers – it's thanks to you that others can enjoy these books in the best presentation possible!

And for all the writers of Regency Historical Romance, whose books I read, who inspired me to write in this fascinating period.

Chapter One

London lay under a deep cover of snow, but everyone seemed to share a feeling of carefree happiness. This was the first Christmas after the end of the long Napoleonic Wars. Waterloo, the mother of all battles, had ended with a resounding victory and, after many years spent fighting, the surviving soldiers had returned to their homes. For most, there was much to celebrate this Christmas, and choirs could sing "Glory to God in the highest, and on earth peace, good will toward men!" giving full value to the truth of the joyous words. But for some, that joy was tempered by other concerns…

Offering his arm to his mother, Lady Pendholm, Lord Charlton Edgeworth, Viscount Pendholm, entered Lord Baildon's townhouse. A footman hurried to relieve them of their outer garments.

They joined the receiving line, and soon they were announced, and went on to join the crush in the ballroom.

Their appearance was followed by a sudden hush, after which conversations resumed, with a slight edge to them. Nobody knew a lot about the new Lord Pendholm, who had only recently returned from the wars on the Continent, to resume his life, and to succeed his brother, the former Viscount Pendholm, who had died in a rather scandalous way, almost a year previously.

It was common knowledge, among the *ton*, that the deceased Lord Pendholm had been something of an unsavoury character. His prowess as a gambler was legendary and it was whispered that he had not restricted himself to respectable gentlemen's clubs like White's or Watier's, but had also attended disreputable gaming hells, associating with shady personages, usurers, swindlers, crooks and all manner of riff raff.

Another, darker, rumour circulated among the gentlemen: that the late Lord Pendholm had had a nasty penchant for violence against women. All of the demi-monde had suddenly ostracised him, after he had viciously beaten a famed *soi-disant* French courtesan, and Mrs Tennant, a notorious Abbess, had banned him from her house of pleasure. All these juicy tit-bits were whispered behind fans and in dark corners, while Charlton and his mother circulated amongst the guests.

Lady Pendholm was in her early fifties and still a beautiful woman. She was silver haired and slender and her son knew well that, under an air of refined gentility, she hid the resilience of a steel blade, the same quality that flashed in her greenish brown eyes when she perceived how they were being oh-not-so-very-subtly snubbed by the *ton*.

She lightly squeezed Charlton's arm, a silent warning not to react. Lord Pendholm looked around, to see if any of his friends were there, but he knew that was a forlorn hope.

Hunter Barrington, Duke of Melton, was spending Christmas with his family at Meltonbrook Chase and would arrive later, at the beginning of the Season; Mr Raphael Morton, as a wealthy Cit, was not normally invited to the *ton*'s entertainments, despite the very real fact that he could buy off many an aristocrat, with change to spare; Lord Geoffrey Clarence was undoubtedly suffering under the grinding heel of his brother, Lord Alfred Clarence, Marquess Woodford, who was rather forcefully focussed on educating poor Geoff in his responsibilities as his heir; Lord Barton Seddon and Lord Gerald Otford, Baron Tillingford were off somewhere together, probably buying horses to improve Gerry's stock at his new estates.

Charlton sighed. The unlikely group known as His Majesty's Hounds had formed during the war, as a very select unit, a closely knit association of men of different, and priceless, talents. Their friendship had been forged on the anvil of many harrowing experiences and was invaluable for all of them. It was second nature for each of them to look for the other Hounds when in any difficult situations, or when faced with potential conflict.

And this, his first public appearance at a social function since his return, was making Charlton feel on edge, his perceptions keenly alert, all of his fighting instincts to the fore. He smiled bleakly. This first skirmish, though important, was not decisive by any means.

He had many battles ahead to fight and win, if he wanted his family to regain the social standing they'd once had and which his brother's behaviour had called into question. And win he would, Charlton vowed: Harriet, his baby sister, a lively, spirited, pretty young thing, would not be looked at askance. He was an honourable man, from an honourable line: he would not allow one rotten apple to ruin it for them all.

Something caught Charlton's attention, pulling him out of his thoughts, and into the moment.

Maybe because he was thinking about war, it seemed significant - it was a man, somewhat older than Charlton, a slim, elegant figure, clad entirely in black, with a ruby signet ring on his finger and a sharp, aquiline profile.

It was the ring that created the association in Charlton's mind. It was the same ring, or a very similar one, as one he had once seen on the hand of a man who had been pointed out to him as a French agent. Was it really him? And, if so, whatever was he doing in London, attending a Christmas Ball?

As he considered the puzzle of the mysterious guest, the crowd parted, revealing a young lady standing beside an older one and looking around with a half excited, half scared expression. A simile flashed through Charlton's mind - the shell opens to reveal the pearl.

He paused, looking at her, and the crowd vanished, the noise quieted, time itself stopped. She was petite, but lushly curved, with a heart shaped face, a small pointed chin, a pert upturned nose and a wide brow with perfect, dark, wing shaped eyebrows.

Her skin was as translucent as mother of pearl, her eyes reminded him of the colour of the gentian violets he had once seen on the Swiss Alps, before the war. She was tastefully dressed in a jonquil satin gown, trimmed with white lace, elbow length white gloves and dainty white kid slippers.

A bony lady in Pomona green elbowed him as she moved through the crush, and brought him out of his reverie.

After a perfunctory "Your pardon, my Lady", and without losing track of the unknown enchantress, Charlton looked for his mother, in the hope that she might know her, and therefore be able to introduce him.

Lady Pendholm was talking with her long-time friend Sir Arthur Bowscale, a distinguished gentleman in his sixties, who owned a ramshackle mansion near Pendholm Hall, their country seat, and who, thanks to his acquaintance with a number of influential peers, had been able to smooth over most of the unpleasantness and the scandal following Michael's murder.

Lady Pendholm looked at her son and was surprised to see the normally calm and steady young man fidgeting.

"Did you want to speak with me, my son?" she asked graciously, her expression curious.

"Yes, Mother, if you please. Would you be so kind as to tell me whether you happen to know that young lady over there, the one dressed in jonquil satin?"

Lady Pendholm peered through her quizzing glass.

"The one near the portly lady in slate grey?"

"Yes Mother, that one. Do you know her?"

"Hmmm, no, I do not think so. I have never seen her before, which is strange. I thought I knew almost everybody. The *ton*, after all, is the most parochial group I know. My curiosity is piqued. Come, my son, let us look for our hostess and ask her."

Lady Catharine Baildon, a vivacious and slightly garrulous sixtyish woman, was chatting with Lady Magda Wilmson, and was, when they approached, telling her, in painstaking detail, all about her younger nephew's exploits and vagaries.

"My dearest Sylvia!" she gushed. "How nice to see you again, after your terrible ordeal... and here is Lord Pendholm... What a handsome gentleman you have become, my dear Charlie! Excuse me if I seem overfamiliar, but I saw you in your swaddling clothes and you will allow an old woman her vagaries... So, you are back from the wars, at long last, and high time it was for that beastly Frenchman to be bundled up and sent halfway to nowhere, to live or to die as he pleases... We must find a nice girl for you straight away, my lord, you need to settle down and have a few children of your own... Will it not be a treat, my dear Sylvia, to hold a baby again, all warm and cuddly? I dote on my Eddie's brood... five of them, up to now, and I could swear dear Dorothy - you know, Eddie's wife – is breeding again..." Half amused and half vexed, Lady Pendholm succeeded at last in stemming her friend's seemingly unstoppable flow of words.

"Will you indulge my curiosity, my dear Catharine? You know that I have been out of society for more than twelve months now, in mourning - you must bring me up to date. Nobody is as knowledgeable as you are about what is going on with the *ton*. For instance, who are those two ladies over there? I cannot seem to remember them."

Lady Baildon, who was very short-sighted but too vain to use a quizzing glass, squinted. "The young one in jonquil satin is Lady Odette Marmont, and the older one in slate grey is her aunt, Lady Farnsworth. Poor Odette has no mother to look after her – a tragic death, you know – and Lady Farnsworth - her mother's sister, you know – is chaperoning her. Almost on the shelf, she is. Already twenty-two and not even betrothed. Very shy little mousy thing, not spirited at all. Would you like me to introduce you?"

Lady Pendholm smiled. One could always count on Catharine for a bit of harmless meddling.

"If you would be so kind, I would be delighted, I'm sure."

With the majesty of a frigate under full sail, Lady Baildon ploughed through the crowd, with Charlton and his mother in tow, and reached Lady Farnsworth and Lady Odette.

Seeing their hostess approaching them, Odette opened her eyes wide and seemed on the point of bolting, but Lady Farnsworth put a restraining hand on her elbow and hissed "Are you set on disgracing me, girl? Behave yourself! You are not a cowering, mistreated scullery maid, you are a Lady and like a Lady will you comport yourself. Now, stop fidgeting, stand straight and try to be gracious."

"Good evening, Lady Farnsworth, how are you? I would like to introduce you to a very dear friend of mine, Lady Sylvia Edgeworth, Viscountess Pendholm. And this is her son, Charlton Edgeworth, Viscount Pendholm. You might have heard that his elder brother, the former Lord Pendholm, died of late. They are just out of mourning and re-acquainting themselves with society life."

Lady Farnsworth smiled. She was a formidable looking woman, with a white streak in her dark hair, piercing grey eyes, a strong chin and an imposing Roman nose.

"My dear Lady Pendholm, how do you do? I do feel for you, my dear husband died not long ago and, between war and mourning, we have not been attending society for a long time. Lord Pendholm, I am honoured to meet you. I'm told you are a war hero and that all of us should be grateful to you for having rid us of the Scourge of Europe. May I introduce you to my dear niece, Lady Odette Marmont? She is the daughter of my dear departed sister. She is here with her father, the Comte de Vierzon. French aristocracy suffered many indignities at the hands of the Corsican parvenu and rejoice with us at his defeat."

Odette looked at Charlton and, caught by his gaze, had to restrain herself from staring. He was a very handsome gentleman, with his wavy locks the colour of a ripe chestnut, rich with golden highlights, and his rich, warm chocolate eyes, where golden motes danced, but what Odette perceived was a compelling quality about him, a feeling of energy held on a tight leash, a strong magnetism emanating from the core of his being.

He was the most intensely alive person that Odette had ever encountered.

While Odette and Charlton looked at each other, their wits askew, the older ladies were engaged in a lively chat.

"Do you see the black clad gentleman over there, the one talking with Lord Stanmore? He is Odette's father, the Comte de Vierzon."

Charlton snapped out of his besotted trance and looked at Odette's father. It was with deep disquiet that he recognised the gentleman he had previously noted. A French agent? An enemy spy? Or simply a French aristocrat, reinstated to his rightful standing by Napoleon's defeat?

'It is not my issue to worry about anymore,' he thought. *'Now I have other fish to fry'.* Yet the sense of disquiet remained, even as he found his gaze drawn, irresistibly it seemed, back to the remarkable blue violet of Lady Odette's eyes.

Chapter Two

Charlton was sitting alone at the breakfast table. His mother's lady's maid, Ellie, had informed him that Lady Pendholm was still tired from the previous evening, and would have a cup of chocolate in her room. His sister Harriet had gone for an early morning ride in Hyde Park, accompanied by her governess and a groom, and was not back yet.

Charlton chuckled. Harriet was fretting and fuming because, not being *out* yet, she was still technically a schoolroom miss and her governess, the very strict Miss Carpenter, treated her accordingly. Thus the little minx had set herself the task of being as disagreeable as possible and an early morning ride on a very cold day was undoubtedly part of her harassment campaign. In fact, Miss Carpenter, although she was a very good teacher, was also a very poor rider – yet Harriet knew that she would feel, nevertheless, compelled to fulfil her duties as a chaperone, and ride regardless.

Charlton drank the last of his black coffee, a habit he had picked up in Spain, and stood.

It was time to continue the thankless job of going through the ledgers and records, covering all of Michael's dealings - a task which he was finding increasingly irksome.

Back from war, he had been chagrined to find that his mother, a lady usually brimming with energy, was at the end of her tether.

Of course, she'd had to manage their estates after his brother's death, which alone would be a strain for her, in addition to dealing with her existing responsibilities. And, of course, the manner of Michael's death, itself, had taken its toll, but, while examining his brother's papers other, much uglier, possibilities for his mother's strained state came to his mind.

They were richer than they had ever been before, this was true: unlike poor Richard, Hunter's now deceased brother, Michael had been a very successful gambler and had not depleted their coffers. However, a very unpleasant pattern was emerging from his ledgers, a disturbing pattern, crooked enough to sicken Charlton (or anyone with a particle of honour, for that matter).

It was clear that Michael's dealings included connections with a number of usurers, some of them quite infamous, and it looked as if the same usurers had granted loans to many a victim of Michael's prowess at the card table.

It was very cleverly hidden between the lines, but Charlton was beginning to suspect that his brother had reaped a double profit: one from his debtors and one, in the form of a hefty percentage, from the usurers in recognition of the value of 'customers' that he had introduced to them.

Such shady dealings were unworthy of a gentleman, and deeply offensive to Charlton's finely honed sense of honour.

Nothing in his brother's business was openly illegal, of course - Michael was far too canny to fall into obvious traps, or to run the risk of being blackmailed by some of his less savoury acquaintances, but, as a whole, his transactions were unethical to say the least.

Charlton sighed and looked out of the window.

Out on the square, the sun was sparkling upon the icicles wreathing the trees and somehow the winter light, with its blue hues, recalled to his mind Lady Odette's eyes, those deep blue eyes in which violet lights danced, like in a pre-dawn sky in high summer. The colour was so unusual, so intense, that it had captured his attention immediately when he had first seen her, and drawn him in, instantly.

He had danced with her, the previous evening, and it had been like stepping into a dream.

She had demurred at first, not because she was playing the coy maiden, but because – quite unbelievably, in Charlton's opinion – she thought that he was offering to dance with her only out of kindness, and had actually said as much, in so many words.

"Do not feel obliged to ask me to dance, my Lord, if you do not feel like it. I am perfectly happy looking at people, you see. They offer an unending field of speculation, if one is of a mind to pay attention. One can imagine stories, plots and secrets or one can turn them into characters in an unending comedy. It can be very absorbing, you know."

"My dear Lady Odette," he had answered her, quite bluntly "I have spent the last years obeying orders and doing things which I often disliked doing. Now I am set on indulging myself. I asked you to dance with me because I would very much like to do so and not, rest assured, because of some misplaced sense of chivalry."

She had smiled, a wonderful, open smile, revealing her even pearly teeth, had curtsied and had held out her hand.

"That being the case, my Lord, I shall be happy to dance with you."

And dance they did, around and around, letting the lilting music of the waltz lead them in intricate swirls and patterns, the lights, and colours and scents drifting around them in a dizzying kaleidoscope.

She felt so light and so alive in his arms, a smile on her upturned face, her scent, a subtle blend of exotic spices and roses, wafting around her.

She was beautiful, it was true, but her beauty was only the outer layer of the attraction she held for him. There was something in her that appealed to him in a deeper and rather disconcerting way. They had exchanged only a few words, but he had felt a sudden affinity with her. Was it the amused curiosity with which she looked at the *ton* and at its whims? Or was it her being an outsider, someone who did not completely belong? Rather as he no longer felt that he completely belonged.

Charlton's reverie was interrupted by another image: a black clad gentleman, an aquiline profile, a ruby, like a drop of blood on his hand.

Lady Odette's father, the Comte de Vierzon.

It was perfectly possible that he was not the French agent his comrade had pointed out to him in Paris. It could be a likeness, even a strong likeness, nothing more. For all he knew, the French agent and Lady Odette's father could even be related, without being in any way connected in their activities.

But something in his mind, some sixth sense developed during his years as one of His Majesty's Hounds, discarded all of the above feeble excuses as mere balderdash. He was certain, deep down certain, of it: Lady Odette's father and the French spy were one and the same.

And, given Charlton's interest in the young lady, this was a setback, to say the least.

His musings were interrupted by a discreet tap on the door.

It was Clarick, the footman, with a silver salver in his hands.

"A letter for you, my lord. An answer is requested."

Charlton stood and took the letter from the salver, broke the seal, and perused it quickly.

"Thank you, Clarick. Please tell whoever is waiting for the answer that I will be there as soon as possible."

"Of course, my lord," the footman bowed and left, while Charlton looked at the missive with a perplexed frown. Why on earth should Lord Cecil Carlisle, Baron Setford, ask for him to call on him in all haste?

Lord Setford was a long-time acquaintance of his, the military spymaster to whom the Hounds had reported, and the mastermind of many a daring enterprise.

He had a deceiving appearance, being little more than five feet five in his stockinged feet, with thinning ash blond hair and delicate hands. Only his eyes, of a piercing light grey, rimmed in black, betrayed his steely will and his superior intellect.

One of the Hounds – probably Geoffrey, who, being a second son, had originally been supposed to enter the Church, and had consequently had a classical education at Oxford – told them once that Julius Caesar was said to have had eyes like Lord Setford's, and Charlton did not doubt it. Behind his unassuming exterior, there was a formidable and devious mind, and a strategist of nigh superhuman ability.

Half an hour later, Lord Setford welcomed Charlton with a smile.

"Sorry to have dragged you from home on such a devilish cold day, Lord Pendholm. Please be seated. May I offer you some refreshment to atone for my solecism?"

Charlton nodded, and sank into the comfortable leather armchair in front of the roaring fire. He had been led to the library, a very masculine room, all nooks and crannies, with large bookcases bearing witness to the somewhat eclectic interests of their owner. His perusal of the room was disturbed by the arrival of a maid.

"Ah, here is your coffee. I am told that you are partial to this beverage, and I share your tastes. Try this blend - I have it sent from Egypt by a local apothecary, who mixes coffee from the Arabian highlands, where it is said that Allah Himself led a weary shepherd to the blessed berries..."

They sat in companionable silence, sipping the aromatic infusion and nibbling on sponge cake.

"Well now, Charlton, if I may call you by your first name, you will be wondering why on earth I asked you to come and see me…"

"Of course you may call me by my first name, Sir, only a few weeks ago you were my senior officer."

Lord Setford guffawed. "I see that I succeeded in teaching you something, did I not? You always were an apt pupil, though. I think that you have, perhaps, already divined the reason for my summons. I need you, Charlton. I need you again, in a different, but no less dangerous field. I cannot force your co-operation, mind you. But I would most deeply appreciate it. It is up to you."

Charlton silently swore. He was cornered and well he knew it. The "up to you" part was simply ludicrous. He would accept whatever task the spymaster saw fit to give him, not because someone or something compelled him to, but because, once a Hound, forever a Hound. If England needed him, well, here he was. And the thrice dratted Lord Setford was perfectly aware of it.

He inhaled and exhaled slowly, like a village wise woman in Spain had taught him, to relieve his edginess. Then he stood, and gave Lord Setford a military salute.

"I'm yours to command, my Lord, Sir."

Lord Setford laughed and applauded.

"Bravo! You wish me to the devil and you are right, but you know where your duty lies. I did not expect anything less from you. Now, sit down, let's have another cup of this excellent coffee and I will tell you everything about it."

Charlton sat as Lord Setford retrieved a portfolio from his desk.

"Now, here we are. We strongly suspect a French spy to be operating in London, with the aim of seducing disaffected Englishmen into becoming Bonaparte's supporters and thus obtaining a repeal of Napoleon's exile to Saint Helena. With him freed, or at least in a much less confined situation, they undoubtedly hope to revive Bonapartism in France, and to start the ugly mess all over again. Even those who did not like Bonaparte much when he was in power may be involved, for it seems they like their newly returned King even less."

"Rather preposterous, Sir."

"Yes, my boy, rather, but, well, there are quite a lot of people who would like to take advantage of an unstable and uncertain situation. There is much social unrest, many soldiers are returning to their homes to find them changed or disappeared, many more are war wounded and without a wage. For those who have no love for the English ruling classes, this is a double chance – they hope to create unrest, or even revolution, here, and to achieve their aims in France as well. Did you read the Two Penny Trash?"

"No, sir, should I?"

"You should rather. Lots of rubbish, of course, but with some important truth mixed in as well, and we should take care to separate the wheat from the chaff, if you ken my meaning. Thus" and he rubbed his hand in a businesslike manner "we have to nip it in the bud."

"Do you suspect somebody?"

"We have a name: the Comte de Vierzon, a French aristocrat who married an English Lady, who is unfortunately deceased. They had a daughter, who was raised, these later years, by her maternal aunt, a Lady Farnsworth. Do you happen to know any of them?"

Hearing the name, Charlton froze. He was right, then. His instinct had not failed him

Charlton told Lord Setford about it, and he nodded, unsurprised.

"Well, Charlton, see you get to know him better. Bring your social graces up to snuff. Try to glean what he is thinking. Your sister Harriet is going to debut soon, isn't she? Invite the Comte de Vierzon, his daughter, and his sister-in-law to the celebration. Flatter the Viscountess. Engage the daughter in light flirtation. I hope she is not an antidote, hmm?"

Charlton could not help but smile.

"If you know that my sister is going to debut soon and that coffee is my favourite hot drink, then am I right to think that you know very well that Lady Odette is not an antidote?"

Lord Setford laughed outright.

"Better for you, my boy, better for you. I am most mightily pleased with your way of thinking. Report to me as soon as you have some interesting information. Good hunting, my Hound."

Chapter Three

Odette and her aunt were sitting in the morning room, chatting amiably about the previous evening's Ball.

Lady Farnsworth, who had a rather caustic sense of humour, was making short shrift of many a lady they had met.

"Did you notice Lady Merriman's gown, my dear? It was a sartorial malapropism. Lime green looks good only with very fair complexions, not with sallow ones. The poor woman looked exactly like a tree frog. One almost expected her to shoot out her tongue and gobble a passing fly. I do not know what her couturière was thinking of. And poor Miss Minton, with those ridiculously tall blue and green feathers stuck in her hair? She looked like a half plucked peacock."

Odette giggled. Her aunt's ability to wittily tear to shreds other people's sartorial choices, whilst keeping a serious, and somewhat stern, face was a constant source of amusement.

Lady Farnsworth gave her a half smile.

She was really very fond of her niece, a very pretty girl with a good head on her shoulders, who needed only to overcome her unfortunate shyness to be assured of being a success in the upcoming Season.

"The jonquil satin you wore yesterday was very becoming, I must say, my dear. Many a young gentleman looked at you with interest, I hope you noticed it."

"Really, Aunt, I think you are flattering me. There were many young ladies far prettier than me..."

Lady Farnsworth rolled her eyes and huffed.

"God give me patience. The dratted girl is set on turning into an old maid. Do you ever look at yourself in the mirror, you silly little goose?"

Odette blushed. She knew she was passingly good to look at, but somehow she did not really believe that anybody could find her interesting. Lord Pendholm, now... she smiled, thinking of him and of his answer to her reticence, so direct as to border on rudeness, yet so refreshing after the manner of the other gentlemen that she had met.

Lady Farnsworth looked at her with her shrewd grey eyes.

"And did you find any of the gentlemen you danced with interesting, my darling?"

Odette thought about it. Other than with Lord Pendholm, she had danced with Sir Larraby, a pimply young man who was apparently only capable of speaking about horses, with Lord Camelforth, a hard featured man with a knowing smile and with Lord Ramsey, a Scotsman with a head of flaming red hair who spoke with an almost unintelligible Highland burr.

"Not really, Aunt. Besides, I did not dance with many gentlemen, did I? Mostly I was a silent witness to the revelry. Sometimes I feel like a spy in a foreign country."

Lady Farnsworth shook her head.

"You are too fanciful, my dear. You should spend less time hidden in the library, perusing musty old volumes. It is not healthy for a young woman to live like a recluse. You should ride in Hyde Park, you should have friends of your own age, you should be carefree and merry. I know," and she fondly patted her niece's knee, "you underwent many a sad experience. You were compelled to leave France, you lost your mother and your grandfather… But this doesn't mean that you should not be happy, all the same. So do tell me - did you not like even the very handsome Lord Pendholm? Even a tiny bit?"

Odette blushed and laughed, without answering her aunt's pointed question.

She sobered suddenly.

"It is true that I miss my mother, Aunt, and sometimes I miss France as well. But you have been so very good to me and I really like it here in England - Aunt, can I ask you something?"

"Of course, my dear, do tell me…"

Odette sighed.

"I am very worried about my father, Aunt. He is so different from the merry, smiling, energetic man I remember. He is bitter, brooding; he hardly speaks to me, as if we were estranged. Why is that, Aunt? I know that he still grieves for Mother, but I would have thought he would have been happy to see me again, and alas, it seems it is not so."

Lady Farnsworth looked thoughtfully at her niece. The girl was far too clever for her own good. Many young ladies had only a very formal relationship with their fathers, and would not have noticed such a change in their demeanour. But she was right - poor Jean-Baptiste had not been the same since his dear wife's demise, it was true, but his wounds went deeper than that. She had had words with him about his attitude, when she had tried to talk him out of his despondency.

"My dear sister-in-law," he had replied with a haughty sneer, "it is very easy for you to speak, when war never reached *England's green and pleasant land*, as the poet has it. You live in peace and have always lived in peace. You did not see your country torn apart, you did not lose your legacy, your dignity, your honour to a nobody from Corse, who had the gall to call himself Emperor. You, and all of the lazy, effete, spendthrift, useless British aristocracy kept everything of yours, while we lost everything of ours. And now we are here, exiled from our own country, waiting for that Bourbon puppet, Louis 18th, to decide whether we are traitors or martyrs. Did you know, my dear sister-in-law, that a group of French noblemen approached your Iron Duke, Wellington, on his way to Paris and asked him to allow them to choose another, worthier King for our beloved country? And did you know that Wellington naysaid them, because it was much better for Great Britain to have a fat, useless, childless old man as the King of France?"

So great had been the bitterness and the scorn with which the Comte de Vierzon had delivered his tirade, that Lady Farnsworth, valiant though she was, had not been able find it in herself to reply.

Remembering, she sighed and took her niece's hand in a heartfelt sign of affection.

"Do not work yourself into a state, my dear. Your father loved your mother very much. It is natural for him to mourn her, even after all these years. But he loves you as well, be sure about it. Have patience, be a dutiful and affectionate daughter and you will see, he will be back to normal in next to no time, believe me."

Odette nodded in acquiescence, but, deep down in her heart, she knew that something was very, very wrong with her father.

Later in the afternoon, when the light faded as the short winter day was coming to an end, Odette went to the library, which had always been her favourite room, everywhere she had lived. But the library in her aunt's house was her favourite of favourites.

It had a cavernous appearance, with its dark oak panels, its maroon velvet curtains and its thick carpets.

Her uncle, Lord Farnsworth, had been a scholar with a particular interest in natural history and geography, while her aunt was an avid novel reader. Her mother, something of a *bas bleu*, was interested in the Classics and was fluent in French, Italian and German.

Odette had always been fascinated by literature and by books in general. She was a compulsive reader and, having inherited her mother's flair for languages, she could read virtually everything the library contained. It was like having the whole world in only one room, she told herself.

This evening she would read something light and entertaining, such as Mansfield Park, one of Miss Jane Austen's novels, whose subtle humour and well-rounded characters made for a relaxing evening's reading.

But, try as she might, the intricate plot, and Fanny's adventures with her wicked cousins, did not seem able to hold her attention. Her mind was continuously straying away to the waltz she had danced with Lord Pendholm.

She had not fooled her aunt, she knew that well. Lady Farnsworth was far too needle-witted to be led astray and had figured out whom she was really interested in. And she was interested; there was no doubt about it.

It was very strange, because, at first, she had thought him an intense, yet otherwise unremarkable, if perfectly proper, gentleman. Then, when he had coaxed her into dancing with him, and had whirled her away, she had realised that he was very remarkable indeed. He had the warmest eyes she had ever seen, the same rich colour as melted chocolate, with tiny motes of gold dancing in them. When he smiled – and he had often smiled while they were dancing – little creases appeared at the corners of his eyes, making him seem both merry and wise, like somebody used to looking at wide, sunny horizons.

She had felt, most intensely, the warmth of his hand, lightly pressing against her back during the waltz, she had smiled at him, she had inhaled deeply of his smell - a fresh, clean, sharp smell recalling to her mind pine forests and sea washed shores.

'Get a grip on yourself, Odette,' she told herself. *'You are no schoolroom miss to become all starry eyed over a gentleman you danced with but once.'*

Totally unbidden, another thought came to Odette's mind: what would it be like to dance with Lord Pendholm – with Charlton, she believed he was named – again? An image formed in her mind - a starlit terrace, a silver moon on the rise, music playing softly somewhere, a heady scent of blooming roses and honeysuckle, and herself, clad in floating silver, swirling dizzily in Charlton's arms.

The book dropped to her lap, and she stared unseeing at the shelves, her imagination carrying her away from the library entirely.

Chapter Four

Sitting in his favourite armchair in his study, Charlton was perusing "The Political Register", better known among its detractors as the "Two Penny Trash", a pamphlet edited by one Corbett. It contained a long, rambling letter to the Chancellor of the Exchequer, which, despite its flamboyant bombast, pointed out several very true facts, such as the financial consequences of the war, the destitute condition of many discharged soldiers, the growing tax burden in Britain and the general disquiet among the poorer citizens.

Charlton folded the pamphlet and sighed.

The situation was rife with danger. It would be very easy for a determined and crafty agitator to find allies among the discontented middle class, who were disgusted by the conspicuous consumption of Prinny's court, and among the young bucks, who were easily inflamed by romantic rhetoric and the promise of heroic feats. That would be a ramshackle collection, to be sure, but a potentially disruptive one.

Add a careful dab of blackmail (an easy enough endeavour, given the number of skeletons hidden in the *ton*'s closets), the right amount of gold in the right pockets, some pressure brought to bear on the right people, and the cauldron would come to a boil, if not stopped in time. And the Comte de Vierzon was in the thick of it, no doubt about it, Charlton was sure of it.

During his years as a Hound, he had developed an uncanny sixth sense for suspicious characters, and the Comte was undoubtedly one of them.

Well, at least his delicious daughter was in the clear. She had been in England since she was little more than a child, under the tutelage of the highly respectable, and very formidable, Lady Farnsworth, who, while openly acknowledging her brother-in-law, the Comte de Vierzon, had seemed, to Charlton, to be slightly wary of him, enough so that her reaction warranted a closer look.

Charlton smiled ruefully. A good excuse to pay a visit to Viscountess Farnworth and, incidentally, to the beautiful Odette who, despite his many troubling duties, had never been very far from his thoughts.

~~~~~

A knock at the door announced his mother, with whom he had fallen into a pleasant pattern.

They would meet in the evening, in front of a good fire, in the secluded cosiness of her private parlour, and talk.
~~~~~

They would exchange bits of gossip, his mother being endowed with a sparkling wit and a sharp eye for the goings on of society life, and then they would almost inevitably turn to more serious topics.

He had found, to his delight, that his mother was a wonderful listener, very skilfully and gently encouraging her son to unburden himself about his years as His Majesty's Officer. At first, he had been afraid to frighten, shock or offend her delicate sensitivity with his gruesome stories, but he had quickly learned that the Viscountess Pendholm, despite her seemingly frail beauty, had an inner core of strength and a compassionate heart that made it easy to lay one's burdens down upon her shoulders.

He was also beginning to discover how hard the last years had been for his mother.

She did not wail and moan, as many other women would have done, but Charlton realised that Lady Pendholm had not been unaware of his deceased brother's unethical business methods, as he had rather, for her sake, hoped. Up to now, she had only hinted at what she knew, and perhaps had seen, but Charlton could not avoid the feeling that she knew much more, and was still uncertain about speaking openly of Michael's misdeeds.

The right time would come, though. They were still learning to know and trust each other again, Charlton often mused. As a young man he had had scant time for his family, what with his years at Eton, then his time as a cadet, when his father, the late Lord Wilfred Pendholm, had bought him a cornetcy, and all these last years as Captain Lord Pendholm.

Through those years, the very idea of being friends with his mother would have seemed preposterous to him.

Now, here he was, sitting in a very comfortable armchair, in his mother's exquisitely appointed parlour and, instead of being overwhelmed by this very feminine environment, he felt soothed and peaceful.

They were sipping a glass of mellow Port wine, and staring in amiable silence at the flames dancing in the fireplace.

Charlton looked surreptitiously at his mother and was shocked to discover that her cheeks were wet with tears. He stood up and put a concerned arm around her shaking shoulders.

"What is it, Mother? What ails you? How can I help?"

"Oh, Charlton, how can I tell you? I am so very ashamed..." she sobbed, holding to him and hiding her face against him.

"It is about Michael, is it not? I feared as much. What did he do to distress you so badly, even now? Please, Mother - tell me! I am here to relieve you of your worries, not to add to them!"

Lady Pendholm looked up into her son's eyes and saw love, anxiety and concern but, most of all, she saw an upright, honourable man, who would do what was right, whatever the cost.

She smiled, a little shakily, dabbing at her tears with a lace handkerchief.

"You are a good boy, a good son and you will be a good Viscount Pendholm, much better than your brother, God have mercy upon his sinful soul, could ever have been. You are right - Michael's wicked ways still haunt me. It is about the girls..."

Rather bewildered, Charlton looked at his mother.

"The girls?"

"The maids, Charlton. Your brother… how can I put it?… abused them. Oh, I know, I'm no fool, I know that taking advantage of maidservants is quite common and only slightly frowned upon… But your brother delighted in mistreating them… no, mistreating is too light a word for such… wanton cruelty. He delighted in hurting them, in beating them, in scaring them out of their wits…"

Charlton was horrified. He had long known something was wrong with the way his brother treated the fairer sex. Even when they were children, he had seen little girls - their cousins, mostly – running away from Michael, crying and complaining about having been slapped or pinched, but he had never suspected him capable of such foul deeds.

Now, suddenly, many things made sense, which had not before, for instance, the great difficulty in hiring female staff, maids in particular. It had been a lengthy enterprise to find a lady's maid for Harriet and he had perceived the wariness with which the entire staff was treating him. After all, he was Michael's brother: it could well be that he shared with him a twisted taste for cruelty and abuse. In light of this new revelation, he could not, in any way, blame the staff for their nervousness.

"How long have you known, Mother?"

"I suspected, but I did not know for sure until… until…"

Another sob broke her words, despite her obvious efforts to compose herself.

"Be easy, Mother. You do not need to speak about it, if it makes you suffer so."

Lady Pendholm shook her head.

"It is true, I do not want to speak about it, but I must. Else, how can I make amends, and offer reparation to these poor creatures, and... and... and to their innocent children?"

She straightened up and looked directly into her son's face. Her voice took on an icy clarity and her sweet face turned into a stern marble mask – it was most obvious to Charlton that she was forcing herself to speak.

"Your brother liked the taste of pain and the smell of fear. I know there are women who are not averse to a playful smack or nip or to an... energetic caress... in the bedroom, but Michael treated those poor girls as if they were... things, to use for his pleasure, to beat into submission, to cater to... to his... depravities, to discard without a thought when they ceased to appeal to him. I had noticed bruises, which they tried to explain away, as having knocked into a door or as having absentmindedly hurt themselves while cleaning, but I could not make heads or tails out of it." She paused a moment, shaking slightly as she sat, her eyes wide with a kind of horror. After a few deep breaths, she continued.

"Also, I noticed maids startling, and trying to make themselves scarce, when they heard Michael's voice, maids more often giving notice and finding service elsewhere, without even asking for a written character, and maids refusing to be hired, ever at a higher salary than is customary. But that is not even the worst part, my son." she added grimly.

"I have already told you that your brother did not treat them as human beings. He did not even treat them as he treated his horses or his hounds. He wanted to see them cowering, humiliated, broken, showing the visible signs of his brutality. And he was not careful. He did not care at all. He rutted like the animal he was, God forgive me, and got them with child. I discovered it all when Mary left me. She was my personal maid, a very sweet and pretty girl. I particularly valued her because she was lettered, a rare feature in females of the lower classes, and she was very eager to improve herself. She was a hard-working girl, a good seamstress and she kept everything about me immaculate and in perfect order. She had a natural taste for cleanliness and she… she used to be a merry, lovely innocent, until your brother began to… take an interest in her. "

Again, Lady Pendholm paused, looking at Charlton, but, he suspected, not really seeing him at all – she seemed deep in the memory of what she described, reliving it as she told him the terrible story. Her voice was quite unlike its normal tone as she told him the rest.

"Mary fled one night, to where, no-one knew, and left a note for me, hidden in my journal. It was for my eyes only, do you see? She asked for my forgiveness - my forgiveness, God have mercy! She left because she feared that, if Michael beat her again, she would lose her baby. She loved it already and she would do anything in her power to protect it. She was too ashamed to confide in me and was afraid that I would not believe she had been forced. Yet she could not bring herself to leave without telling me why."

Lady Pendholm was shaking and Charlton, who had listened, speechless, to the account of his brother's nefarious behaviour, took her hands to steady her.

"My dear Charlton, what did I do wrong to give birth to such a monster? I decided, on the spot, to mount a search, because I cannot accept the idea that my grandchildren – even if born out of wedlock and out of spite and carelessness rather than out of love – should live like waifs, doomed to misery and misuse. I hope you agree, because, if you do not, I will pursue my quest all the same."

While saying so, a martial light shone in Lady Pendholm's eyes. Charlton smiled and kissed her hands.

"How could I not bow to the will of such a forceful lady? Mother, I am on your side. I will not stand by and see any baby with the blood of this family in its veins go wanting, nor its mother. This, I do solemnly swear. Now, tell me. How have you conducted your search – for I believe that is what you are telling me – that you have been searching?"

"I took Sir Arthur Bowscale into my confidence, at least partially. I told him that I needed to trace my lady's maid, who had left me without an apparent reason, and asked if he could recommend to me a reliable agent of inquiry for hire. He was very helpful and introduced me to a Mr. Anthony Starling, a former Bow Street Runner who had left employment with the Town to work on his own. I liked him and hired him on the spot. He sent me a message a few days ago to tell me that he believes he has found one of those unlucky girls, and he is going to confirm it tomorrow. I pray to God that he really has found at least one of them, and that it is not already too late."

She shuddered as she continued.

"The winter is bitterly cold, and how could a young girl and her baby survive, without employment, without nourishing food, without a comfortable home?"

Charlton looked at his mother with open admiration. She was really a wonderful woman, brave, compassionate and honest to the core.

"What are you going to do, if he has really found one of them?"

"Well, my son, I have been rather forward, I must admit. I asked my man of business to look for a suitable house, and he found a nice place near Well-close Square. It is a respectable, if not fashionable, address and I believe that the girl Starling found will be perfectly comfortable there. I am going tomorrow to have a look at it. Will you come with me?"

Charlton smiled.

"Of course, Mother. It will be my pleasure. One thing, though: how are you going to pay for it?"

Lady Pendholm defiantly raised her chin.

"With my own allowance, of course." Her tone dared him to argue with her. Charlton grinned.

"As head of the family, I strictly forbid it. My brother left a lot of money: at least some small part of it must be used to amend for his evil ways. All the expenses for your search, and this house, and the girl's ongoing needs, will be paid for from the estate. And this, my lady Mother, is my last word on the matter."

"I see that, as a mere female, I have to submit to your masterful decree. So be it. Good night, my son. I am proud of you."

And Lady Pendholm left the room, a tender smile on her lips, feeling better than she had for at least four years.

Chapter Five

The house was well situated, in a respectable street, on the fringes of the fashionable part of London. On the corner, a pie-seller was hawking his wares, bundled up in a voluminous greatcoat and a bright red muffler. The round face of a young girl was peeping out of a nearby window. A lady in a burgundy cloak was hurrying home and, as she opened the door, a sweet smell of baking apples wafted out. A little farther on, there were some shops: a haberdasher, a baker, a butcher, and a small public house.

It was very quiet, without the rush of carriages, horses and people that was common in the central streets of the thriving metropolis. The house looked sturdy and well built, with a rather large garden and a kitchen garden at the back.

Lady Pendholm looked at her son.

"What do you think, Charlton? Will it do?

"Let's have a look inside, Mother. I would like to see how many rooms there are and to check the state of the kitchen. Come!"

Mr Swithin, Lady Pendholm's man of business, produced a key and they went in without further ado.

~~~~~

Meanwhile, in a wretched house in Dyott Street, a few yards from St. Giles-in-the-Fields' Church, a young woman was trying to patch up a broken window with paper and rags, in the desperate attempt to keep out the sharp wind mixed with sleet. Her hands were blue with cold and barely able to perform the apparently simple task. She did her best, but the window was in such bad repair as to make her attempt almost guaranteed to be in vain. She sank onto a low bench, covered her face with her hands and broke into tears.

Another woman, a few years older, hurried over.

"Shush, love, please do not give up! Do it for your baby!"

"It is useless, Rose..." the young woman sobbed. "She will die, just as Annie's baby died. She was such a pretty little girl, but she took ill and died in a few days, did you not know? How can a little 'un survive, with no warm fire, no good food, in such a horrible winter? She will die, and I will die with her and it will be for the better. What sort of life can I offer her, anyway?"

The older woman held her close, and sighed.

Her sister, under a meek and retiring appearance, was as stubborn as a mule and as proud as the devil. Why could she not appeal to the great Lady she had once been maid to? Rose had asked her more than once, but Mary had answered that she would not, for her life, risk to meet that awful Lord Michael once more.
~~~~~

And when the news of his murder got to them, she still would not go.

"My lady would not believe me. Not now, with her son just dead in such a terrible way. She would not believe anything wrong about him. And what about his brother, the new Viscount Pendholm? What if he is as bad as his brother was? These things run in families, you know…"

Rose held her sister closer and grimly consigned Lord Pendholm and all his breed of good-for-nothing parasites to the nethermost hell, there to burn for the rest of eternity.

Out in the street, below the broken window, among the dirty snow, a burly man in worn clothes and dirty boots was looking at the house with a knowing smile and muttering to himself.

"I found them. I am sure, now. I can give Lady Pendholm the good news and collect my reward. Also, I can assure her that the girl is very poor, but also very respectable. Such a Lady would not want to help a common slut and her brat… As to why the girl ran and whose child her baby is, one is entitled to one's ideas…"

~~~~~

Inside, the house was cold and smelled musty. Dust covered everything with a thick layer and cobwebs hung in festoons from the ceilings.

Lady Pendholm fastidiously raised her skirts, in what was probably a forlorn hope of avoiding soiling the hem with the dirt.
~~~~~

"One cannot see a thing in this gloom. Will you open the windows, Charlton? And maybe light the fire? Is that not a coal scuttle, over there, near the fireplace?"

"Good idea, Mother. We shall see if the chimney has a good draft or is clogged. I won't ask you to sit down, everything is filthy and in need of a good scrub!"

Mr Swithin scurried to Charlton's side, trying to prevent him from performing such a menial job as lighting a fire, but Viscount Pendholm shooed him away.

"During the war I was often my own cook, my own groom and my own servant, Mr Swithin. Nothing new to me, rest assured..."

Having got the fire going, and seeing that the chimney had a perfect draft, Lord and Lady Pendholm started to explore the house, which was ample enough to welcome a largish family. There was a good dry basement, lighted by several small windows, and by a door opening onto the kitchen garden. It accommodated a large kitchen, a pantry, a servant's sitting room, a laundry room, a cellar and a scullery with its boiler and its cistern. The water was piped and, though dusty, everything seemed in good order.

The hall, the dining room, the parlour, and the drawing room were on the ground floor; the first floor contained two large bedrooms, two smaller bedrooms, two spacious closets and a large, airy nursery with a smallish side-room for the nurse.

The servant's rooms were in the attic and there was, also, an airing room where the washing up could be hung to dry, and where food, like apples, would keep for a long time.

Lord Pendholm looked at his mother and nodded.

"Very well, Mr Swithin, buy the house, have the furniture checked and completed and the needful repairs done. Hire what staff you deem necessary and see that everything is in order before the week ends. We may need the place straightaway and I want it available as soon as possible."

"Yes, my Lord, everything will be done to your satisfaction, I'm sure."

"Good. Let's go back home, Mother, it is starting to snow."

While travelling home in their comfortable carriage, a hot brick at his feet, Charlton felt distinctly uneasy.

There was something about the house –its address, maybe? - that was nagging at him, something he should know but just could not remember, something flickering at the edge of his memory like an elusive will-o'-the-wisp.

What with all the papers that Lord Setford had given him, plus his brother's official and unofficial ledgers, he had had his fill of dubious characters, shady dealings, suspects and flimsy evidence. Perhaps all of that was making everything seem odd or suspicious to him.

It will come to me, Charlton thought and wished, not for the first time, for his friend Hunter's skill in seeing a pattern in a disparate, haphazard jumble of facts, names and pieces of information.

Hunter had tried to explain his methods to his fellow Hounds, claiming that they were, in fact, very simple and based on mere logic, but to no avail.

There was something uncanny in his skill, a nigh on supernatural intuition, the ability to see, recognise and take into account apparently negligible details, and bring them together to discover the whole of something hidden.

Charlton smiled, thinking about his friends and hoping to be able to see them all soon, as he tried to silence the obstinate little voice that was whispering in his mind, and telling him that he was missing something very important.

Chapter Six

Standing beside a cheval mirror, Lady Farnsworth was critically supervising her niece's toilette. The dressing room was lavishly appointed in the Chinese style, which was all the rage after the Regent had thus furnished his Pavilion in Brighton. A delicate black lacquered table held an assortment of lotions and perfumes, while a similar cabinet overflowed with ribbons, lace, ostrich feathers and other fashionable trinkets and baubles.

Odette's long, thick dark tresses, which she had refused to cut, were arranged in a simple but becoming style, braided with silver ribbons in a high crown and calling attention to the fine carriage of her head and her graceful neck.

Her gown was pale blue, with sapphire and silver trimmings, small puffed sleeves and a low cut bodice. Sapphire earrings and a thin gold chain with a sapphire pendant were her only jewellery.

Odette looked anxiously at her aunt.

"Is this dress not cut a bit too low, Aunt? After all, it is a dinner party, not a Ball…"

"Balderdash." Lady Farnsworth replied. "You look ravishing, if I do say so myself. Your lady's maid is a very accomplished hairdresser, this coiffure is flattering to your complexion and gives you added height. And stop fretting about your gowns being cut too low or too close-fitting. You are not a schoolroom miss anymore, Odette. You are a young lady on the marriage mart and your aim is to get married. A bit harsh, spoken out like that, I know, but there it is." Lady Farnsworth smiled as she spoke, taking the edge off her words.

"To that end, a word to the wise, my dear: try to practice light banter, witty repartee, sweet smiles and fluttering lashes and do not try to engage young men on serious topics such as literature, history or art. Men are wary of intelligent women. They need to feel in charge. They need to feel worldly wise, experienced and knowledgeable. A sweet, naïve girl enhances those feelings for them, and is thus highly prized. An intelligent, sharp witted woman does not – I think that most of them find intelligence in a woman rather threatening. Remember that! At least, until you are married - after that, you may do as you please."

Odette lowered her eyelids, fringed by long, black, curling lashes.

"Yes, Aunt, I will take to heart your kindly advice. I know I cannot be dependent upon you much longer. You have granted me this Season and I am determined to make the most of it."

Lady Farnsworth snorted and shook her head.

"God give me patience. Do not be a ninnyhammer, my girl! I want you married for your own good! You know I have no children and now, especially after your dear Uncle's demise, you are a blessing and a joy to me! You may stay with me for as long as you wish, and welcome, and, besides, I am planning to settle on you a comfortable competence, to assure your independence. But it would be much better for you, my dear, if you had a home of your own, a man of your own and your own children to raise, rather than playing lady-in-waiting to an old crotchety woman. By the way," she slyly added "I understand that young Viscount Pendholm will be at the dinner party…"

Odette blushed from head to toe and, against her better judgement, smiled in anticipation.

~~~~~

"Why can I not come with you? It is only a boring old dinner party, after all. I'm fed up with staying at home, being a good girl, going to sleep at eight o'clock and eating all my nice pudding! I'm eighteen! You were already married when you were my age, Mama!"

Harriet was on the verge of tears, her pretty face screwed into a grimace, and she seemed just a step away from throwing a fully-fledged tantrum.

Her brother put his hands on her shoulders and made her turn and look at herself in the mirror.
~~~~~

"Look at your face, Harriet. Is this the countenance of a young Lady? Does it show the restraint, the self-control, the graceful manners, that a young Lady should possess? No, it does not. This is the face of a spoiled brat - of a spoiled, snotty brat, at that. Go wash your face, retire to your room and if I hear one single whisper to indicate that you have continued to carry on in this disgraceful fashion, I'll pack you back to Pendholm Hall and we will not speak again about your coming-out until next year."

Harriet looked at her brother's stern face, glared at him and turned to her mother with pleading eyes, but Lady Pendholm was unmoved. "Your brother is perfectly right. Up to your room you go now, and do not let me hear from you until tomorrow."

At a loss for words, Harriet ran up the stairs, covering her face with her hands. Charlton and Lady Pendholm heard the sound of a door being forcefully slammed shut, and could not help laughing softly.

"You are right, you know, Charlton. Harriet really is a spoiled brat. She is my last child and the only girl, she has always been indulged considerably more than was right and reasonable. Moreover, these last months since Michael died, I have had so much to worry about, that I have been remiss in my duty to your sister. A good, stern lecture is long overdue. I shall talk with her tomorrow."

"Do not chide yourself, Mother. Harriet was spoiled by us all, myself included. She is an intelligent girl, though. After she has brooded and pined away for a while, and imagined herself the persecuted heroine in those trashy novels she likes, she will come around, you will see."

Lady Pendholm gratefully squeezed her son's arm.

"Thank you, Charlton. Now, if you are ready, we should go. Being late is considered fashionable, but in my opinion it is simply rude, especially at a dinner party."

~~~~~

During the journey to Lord and Lady Coreley's dinner party, Charlton fell to brooding and, looking at his frown, his mother let him be. He was thinking about the Comte de Vierzon, and about the progress he was making in gaining his trust. He had to keep the underlying dislike he felt for the Frenchman under strict control, yet he could not but admit that it was a dislike mixed with reluctant admiration.

The fellow was a born conspirator. He never spoke openly, he never clearly set forward his plans and he never uttered a single word that could be construed as open sedition. Nevertheless, his resentment against England, and the English aristocracy in particular, seeped into each one of his sentences. He was sharp as a blade, unprincipled, dangerous, and charismatic. Little wonder that so many young bucks, second sons, and impoverished noblemen had fallen under his spell.

Charlton had played the part of the clean-cut, upright military man, who, back from war, had discovered that injustice was running rife in England and was horrified by it. It was very easy to fall into character, because, to some extent, he was actually living a similar situation, albeit at a personal level, and the Comte of Vierzon had no inkling of what he really was about.
~~~~~

Charlton was so deep in his thoughts that he did not realise they had arrived until Lady Pendholm gently shook him out of his musings.

~~~~~

They were received in the rather opulent foyer, where a footman relieved them of their outer garments and led them to the drawing room, where the guests were waiting for dinner to be announced.

Lady Coreley, a charming and witty woman in her mid-thirties, greeted them warmly.

"My dear Lady Pendholm, Lord Pendholm, I am so glad you could come. This is not a large party, there will be time enough during the Season for grand squeezes, but I hope you will find the other guests interesting. A cosy affair with a few chosen friends is the best way to while away a winter evening, do you not agree?"

Charlton smiled. He was starting to feel that the wind was changing and that the *ton* was beginning to realise how different he was from his late brother. He attended only unimpeachable establishments, was scrupulously honest in all his dealings and the *on-dit* of recent days had included the fact that he had cut, completely, many of Michael's least savoury associates, who were trying to trade on that acquaintance in the hope of associating with him. Lady Coreley herself led them to the dining room, where some of the guests were already gathering, a distinct sign of esteem and trust.
~~~~~

"Lady Pendholm, will you do me the honour of sitting near me? And, Lord Pendholm, you are to sit near Lady Odette Marmont - you are already acquainted with her, I believe."

~~~~~

Sitting beside Odette, Charlton found himself to be totally captivated by her.

She was shy, but not coy. Her eyes sparkled as if she was contemplating something amusing which only she could see. Charlton tried to gently draw her out, to find a subject which she could find interesting. At last he started to talk about the Elgin Marbles and how they had been taken away from the Parthenon in Athens.

"I saw them in 1811, when they were first displayed. Now I hear that the British Museum is going to purchase them. I hope it is so, such beauty should be shared with everybody, not just be the private property of a single individual."

Odette blushed becomingly.

"Did you really see them, Lord Pendholm? Tell me about them, please! I have heard many discordant opinions: some said that they are little more than rubble, scarcely worth the trouble, others, instead, have hailed them as great works of art. What do you think?"

"I heartily agree with the second opinion. The Parthenon marbles really are a wonderful work of art. They brought to my mind the great Greek and Latin classic literature, The Odyssey, the Aeneid, the Iliad..."
~~~~~

"Sing, Muse, the fatal wrath of Peleus' son/which to the Greek unnumbered evils brought/and many heroes to the realms of night/sent premature and gave their limbs a prey/to dogs and birds, for such the will of Jove/when fierce contention rose between the chiefs/Achilles and Atriedes king of men..."

Charlton stared at her. She was glibly reciting the introduction to the Iliad, and somehow the ancient, solemn syllables sounded perfectly right on Odette's lovely lips.

Suddenly she stopped, looked at him wide-eyed, and blushed a furious crimson.

Charlton smiled at her, with some dismay at her ceasing what was a marvellous rendition of the words.

"Why did you stop? It was a very good rendition. Is it Reverend Morrice's translation?"

She looked at him, her eyes alive with a strange mixture of embarrassment and mischief. "Are you not shocked? Young ladies are scarcely expected to toss off Homer's verses at random."

"I am delighted, rather. I find myself bored by inconsequential chit-chat, silly giggles, and coy maidens batting their eyelashes at me, then producing ugly watercolours for me to admire."

Odette gave him a full, sparkling smile that transformed her face and quite took his breath away. By Jove, he thought, but she was quite an astoundingly beautiful girl...

"Indeed, I hope not to shock you if I tell you that my only regret is not to be able to read Homer in his original language..."

"Well, I read the classics at Eton. I was a second son, you know, so it was the Church or the Army, for me. I chose the Army, but I did not forget my youthful efforts to learn Homer's language - I could teach you, if you truly wish…"

Odette was bewildered. Here was a gentleman who not only was not distressed by her love for literature and languages, but who was also, it seemed, willing to help her become even more learned.

She looked at him doubtfully. "Are you teasing me?"

"Not at all. Do you read Latin, by chance?"

"A little. I am better acquainted with modern languages: French, German, Italian…"

Charlton was enchanted all over again by this evidence that she was far more than a typical boring society miss, and, in his delight at her quick intelligence, he put aside his misgivings about her very dangerous father.

~~~~~

From the opposite side of the long table, the Comte de Vierzon looked at Lord Pendholm through slitted eyes.

He would be a worthy addition to his plot, that one. His military experience would not come amiss, and he had also a good head on his shoulders. He could even like him, were he not a member of the hateful British aristocracy. The Comte's calculating black eyes skimmed over Odette. It was clear that she liked Lord Pendholm and, to judge from the besotted smile on his face, he liked her in return.
~~~~~

The Comte sneered slightly, irritated by the sight. An attachment between those two was to be discouraged, it would not do at all. He would not bestow his beloved child on someone who was a valuable tool in his hands, but an enemy nevertheless. Ah, well, let the cauldron simmer, it would soon come to a boil...

Chapter Seven

In her small cold room, Mary disconsolately looked out of the only surviving pane of a wrecked window. The few hard snowflakes of the afternoon were rapidly turning into a blizzard, and only a few pieces remained of their carefully hoarded coal. Her little girl was sleeping, snug under a pile of ragged blankets and discarded cloaks. In the greyish light of the gathering winter dusk, the young woman was waiting for her sister, who had gone out earlier to deliver her work and receive her meagre salary, hardly enough to support her, let alone another woman and her baby.

'I am shamefully exploiting Rose,' she thought. *'I should do something to earn my daughter's keep and mine, but what can a woman do, without a character? I help her with her sewing, it is true, and of course I can keep house for her, but I do not feel it is enough. And anyway, how can anybody call this hovel "home"? If this wretched weather keeps up, we will not live through the winter - we cannot afford both food and coal...'*

She thought about something her landlady, Mrs Grafton, had told her, and shivered, recalling the avaricious glint in the older woman's eyes.

"Don't be a fool, dearie. You are young, you are pretty, a bit skinny, it is true, but there are gentlemen who would very much appreciate your innocent, waifish air. You could make a good living. Your daughter would not starve. I could find you a better place to stay... When you decide, let me know. You know where to find me."

'When you decide,' not *'if you decide...'* Mary sighed. She could not think of a man touching her without fear and revulsion, but she knew that, if her daughter's life were at stake, there would be no other avenue open to her.

~~~~~

When there were no guests, Charlton liked to dine in the small dining room, which was much cosier than the formal dining room, with its long table and its vaulted ceiling.

The small dining room was beautifully appointed in sage green and cream, with striped curtains in the same colours, a fireplace with a rose marble mantel and a thick Aubusson rug in muted tones of cream, rose, and green.

Harriet was on her very best behaviour, the model of a demure young lady. After having let her sulk in her room for a whole day, Lady Pendholm had, rather brusquely, put an end to what she had labelled 'a disgraceful melodrama' and had thoroughly catechised her wayward daughter.
~~~~~

Charlton also was in a good mood, because, at long last, his friends were back in London and he had been able to spend some time with them the previous evening, after escorting his mother home from the dinner party. He had sorely missed them, and smiled, recalling their friendly banter and outrageous jokes.

Charlton looked at his mother, wondering why she was fidgeting and seemingly anxious. Lady Pendholm played with her food, twisted her napkin and seemed to discourage any attempt at conversation.

Harriet, still smarting from the unusually stern set down, interpreted her mother's apparent agitation as a sign of herself still not being back in favour, and excused herself as soon as she politely could, claiming to have a letter to write to a friend of hers.

Charlton and his mother lingered a bit longer over their coffee and then retired to her parlour for their usual, pleasant after-dinner coze.

As soon as they were comfortably ensconced in their armchairs, with glasses of dark ruby port waiting on the small, mother-of-pearl inlaid table in front of them, Charlton took his mother's hands into his and looked her straight in the eyes.

"What is it, Mother? What is the matter with you? You have not been yourself these past hours…"

A radiant smile lit up her face.

"He found them, Charlton! He found them! He is sure it is them!"

Charlton kissed his mother's cheek, embracing her briefly.

"I feel that I do not need to ask who *'he'* is and who *'they'* are, but would you care to expatiate? Just a little, for your dull boy's sake?"

Lady Pendholm laughed, a silvery, happy sound which Charlton had not heard for a long time.

"Of course, how silly of me! I told you about Mr Starling, did I not? Well, he sent me a note and we met this afternoon. He gave me a detailed written account of his activities and told me that Mary and her baby – a little girl, it seems - are living in a dilapidated tenement house near St. Giles in the Fields' church. They went to stay with Rose, Mary's older sister, a childless widow. She is a seamstress, and supports Mary and her baby with her work."

Charlton frowned.

"At the current rates, I do not see how they can make ends meet. It must be very difficult for them."

She looked at him with eyes brimming with tears.

"Mr Starling told me that they are very poor, but very respectable. He told me that many unfortunate young women, mainly housemaids dismissed without a character, sell their virtue as their only option if they are not to starve… He told me that he had spoken with Rose: she was taking home a heavy basket full of gown material and he offered to help her carry it. Charlton - the poor woman's fingers were swollen with cold and bleeding from needle pricks! And she did not have mittens, only rags wound around her hands! We must go at once! We must save them!"

Lady Pendholm rose, agitated, and went to look out of the window.

"Look, Charlton, it is snowing. And they have no coal, they cannot afford to buy it. And they live in a rented room full of drafts, in a disreputable neighbourhood. Who knows what they eat - or even *if* they have anything to eat? How can I stay here, snug in my beautiful home, replete from a lavish meal, sipping port and looking at the logs crackling in the fireplace, while they lack even the most elementary creature comforts? I cannot stand it!"

"Easy, Mother dear, easy. Of course, we must go, and we shall do so as soon as possible, but we must plan. St. Giles in the Fields is a dangerous part of London. We cannot barge in there with a crested carriage, decked out in our finery. We would be bait for every cutthroat for ten miles around. It would be sheer folly, and I will not risk your safety for anybody's sake. We could not help Mary if we were, ourselves, hurt or robbed."

She gave him a self-conscious smile, recognising the wisdom of his words, but unhappy with the delay regardless.

"You are right, of course. We must plan. What do you suggest?"

"With your permission, I would like to take my friend Geoff into our confidence. He is the best shot that I know and a devil of a swordsman as well. I would ask him to come with us."

"Geoff? Do I know him?"

Charlton smiled, realising how natural it was for him to think of the Hounds by their familiar names, rather than their formal titles.

"Sorry, Mother. You probably know him as Lord Geoffrey Clarence, heir to his brother Alfred Clarence, Marquess Woodford. He is one of the Hounds, you know, I told you about them…"

"Of course, I should have made the connection at once. I am not usually so slow-witted, but I am scared and exhilarated at the same time, and that does not bode well for rational thought. Yes, tell him to come, he sounds like exactly the right man for the job."

"We shall go in a rented hansom, and I will provide suitably shabby clothes for us all. What do you think, Mother, should we ask Mr Starling to come with us?"

"Why yes, of course, Charlton. He knows the address, he is already acquainted with Rose and he is familiar with the neighbourhood. I could ask Gwennie, the scullery maid, to come with us as well. She was Mary's close friend, it should reassure the poor girl to see her."

"Good idea. I will ask Geoff tomorrow morning. Better, I will ask him here for lunch. We shall talk it over together. Could you ask Mr Starling to call in the afternoon? Around half past three, maybe?"

"I shall do so. Also, I shall speak with Gwennie. If you can provide our disguise by tomorrow, we could go that afternoon. Mr Starling told me that Rose is usually back home by five o'clock. I know that it will be already dark, but I would rather they were all there…"

"Perfect. If you think of something else, let me know. I shall do the same." Charlton found himself looking forward to taking action.

It was most pleasant to consider actually being able to begin to put right the terrible results of Michael's behaviour.

Lady Pendholm smiled happily.

"Oh, Charlton, I can hardly wait. Perhaps as soon as tomorrow, I shall see my little one, my grandchild… And all will be well, will it not?"

Charlton hugged his mother and kissed her on her shining silver blonde hair.

"Now let us retire and try to sleep. A long day awaits us tomorrow."

Once in bed, though, Charlton found it impossible to sleep.

His mother's impassioned description of Mary's situation had given him a fresh insight into how dangerous the Comte of Vierzon's conspiracy really was. It reminded him of just how desperate the plight of many of the common people was.

What if the Comte's rag tag collection of romantic fools, discontented and impoverished noblemen, and assorted riff raff, should rouse London's populace to join them? What if a nasty, but circumscribed coup should escalate into a full-blown riot? After all, the French revolution had started like that.

Charlton shivered. While trying to understand how the social situation really stood, he had prowled London's slums, seeing hunger, ignorance, filth, desolation, desperation. What if, fuelled by some demagogue's rhetoric, desperation turned into anger? He had to discover exactly what the Comte was planning, nip his plot in the bud and do it soon.

But what about Lady Odette?

Charlton longed to be with her, to get to know her better, to spend time with her. He would like to take her riding in Hyde Park, take her to visit the British Museum and explore London with her – even with the requisite chaperone, it would be most pleasant to do so.

Lady Odette's sparkling intelligence, her interesting conversation, her outstanding beauty and her gentle wit had captivated him. But her despicable father cast an ominous shade on their friendship. Even if she were innocent of any wrongdoing, and he was certain that she was, once her father was discovered to have treasonously conspired against Britain, she would be disgraced. Even her unimpeachable aunt could be besmirched by such a scandal. The *ton* would surely shun poor Lady Odette, through no fault of her own.

How could he spare her that trauma? How could he keep her from suffering?

Chapter Eight

Saturday dawned cold and clear, after a day of heavy snow. Odette, who had read late into the night, was awakened by a whispered, but vehement argument taking place under her windows. In the clear crisp air, the sound carried.

She left her bed, put on her heavy velvet wrap, and padded to the window, opening the curtains slightly.

She saw her father, as usual impeccable in the unrelieved black he had worn since her mother's death, arguing forcefully with a portly young man who was unknown to her.

"Never, ever again try to come and harass me at my sister-in-law's home. We have assignments, we have places to meet, we have an overwhelming need for secrecy. If you do not understand these simple facts, you are out. I will not have a young *imbécile* blundering about and imperilling us all."

Feeling disturbed, and somewhat puzzled, Odette closed the curtains and went back to bed.

She picked up, and tried to resume reading, the novel 'The Antiquary', by the same author as 'Waverley', which she had hugely enjoyed, but she could not concentrate on the previously absorbing plot.

What was her father up to? Who was the portly young man? And why was there a need for secrecy? She could not, for the life of her, find an answer to these questions, and was deeply disquieted. Her father was a man of passion: what if he had been led, by his resentment and pain, to some irresponsible enterprise? And why did she feel that Lord Pendholm – Charlton – had something to do with it? Although, perhaps she was simply being imaginative – Lord Pendholm seemed always in her thoughts of late, and she smiled wryly, because she could not help putting Charlton's face to the heroes of each novel she read: Mr Darcy, Major Neville, Edmund Bertram...

'Will I meet him again soon? I do hope so...' she thought, recalling his warm, gold flecked chocolate eyes. *'But Father does not like me being friendly with him... Does father know something bad about him, which makes him unsuitable? After all, as on-dit has it, his brother Michael was a very wicked man...'*

~~~~~

It was four o'clock in the afternoon and, even if the day had been clear and sunny, the cold winter night was already falling. Charlton, his mother, Geoff and Gwennie, the scullery maid, were waiting for Mr Starling, who was going to pick them up in a rented hansom cab.
~~~~~

Gwennie was looking round-eyed with shock at her mistress, who was usually dressed with simple but exquisite elegance, but was now bundled up in a drab grey gown, a moth-eaten woollen shawl, a shapeless bonnet, and black boots which were worn at the heels. Lady Pendholm looked at her son and his friend and smiled. "You two look like a pair of out and out ruffians, if I may say so. I would be afraid to meet two such as you in a dark alley."

Geoff laughed. "We must blend with the landscape, Lady Pendholm. Out and out ruffians come a ha'pence a score in the St. Giles in the Fields' neighbourhood.

Charlton spied a hansom cab approaching.

"Here is our ride, ladies and gentlemen. Let's go."

Moments later, the cab rolled on, leaving the animated central streets and heading into the poorer parts of London, to St. Giles in The Fields.

Lady Pendholm looked out of the grimy windows of the cab with increasing distress. "How far do we have to go, Mr Starling?" she asked.

"Not far now, my Lady. Here, lad, turn left now!" he shouted to the hansom driver. "Stop before the arch!"

After a few minutes, the hansom reached its destination and stopped. Geoff and Charlton alighted first, their hands on the very visible hilts of their daggers; Gwennie followed and helped lady Pendholm down. Mr Starling went and sat with the hansom driver, to ensure that he stayed and waited, ready to leave as soon as possible.

"Hope they don't dawdle, lad…" he muttered "The earlier we leave, the happier I'll be."

~~~~~

Mary was sitting on her pallet, with her little girl on her lap. Rose had just returned and she had brought with her some fresh milk, a loaf of bread and a small lump of sugar, which she, greatly daring, had actually filched from her employer's sugar bowl, when she had deigned to offer Rose some hot tea before seeing her out. Using their last coal, they had warmed the milk on a brazier and sopped the bread in it. The sugar was a treat for the baby, who ate the sweet mush with messy relish, then fell into a deep sleep, curled like a kitten in her cocoon of rags..

'We have made it last as long as possible, but now it has ended,' thought Mary, looking at the flickering embers. *'I have no choice: without coal, my daughter will sicken and die before the winter is over. I'll go and speak with Mrs Grafton. Honour and virtue are luxuries I cannot afford anymore.'*

~~~~~

They climbed the rickety stairs, which creaked ominously under their feet. The stairwell was very cold and very dirty, the stench of cheap cooking, refuse and unwashed bodies hanging heavy in the air. Even Gwennie grimaced.

"What an awful place, my lady…" she whispered. "How can poor Mary live here? And with a baby? How can she stand it?"

"We are here to rescue her, Gwennie", Lady Pendholm answered. "Here we are, this is the door Mr Starling described to us. You knock on the door, my girl, she will not worry if she sees a known, friendly face."

Lady Pendholm stood at Gwennie's back, heard the sound of steps approaching and saw the door opening just a slit. Charlton and Geoff were waiting in the shadows of the landing.

"Who goes there?" asked a wary voice from within.

"I'm Gwennie, ma'm, a friend of Mary's that was scullery maid at Lady Pendholm's. Will you let me in?"

Other steps. A baby whimpering. A whispered exchange. Then the door opened completely.

"Gwennie! It really is you! How did you find me?" Mary exclaimed, hugging her friend. Lady Pendholm answered, speaking from behind Gwennie.

"I have been looking for you for a long time, and at last I have found you, Mary, God be thanked."

Mary looked at the shabbily dressed woman beside Gwennie and gasped in surprise, recognising her past employer.

"Lady Pendholm?" Mary's voice was shaky, uncertain.

Hearing that name and seeing two menacing male shadows in the background, Rose rushed forward and tried to close the door, suddenly afraid, but Lady Pendholm was quicker, thrusting through the door.

Charlton and Geoff followed, and soon the whole party was inside the poor room.

Mary was in a turmoil: she fussed around, looking for a chair for Lady Pendholm to sit on, trying to tidy up, apologising for her inadequate lodging and for having nothing to offer, hiding her bewilderment and embarrassment behind inconsequential blather.

Her sister looked suspiciously at the strangers, who had invaded their hitherto safe haven, shooting black looks at the two men in particular. The little girl, awakened by the unusual disturbance, lay in her makeshift cocoon and looked at everybody with owlish round eyes.

~~~~~

Her shame and chagrin notwithstanding, Mary was overjoyed to see Lady Pendholm again. Sheer relief washed over her, when she realised that, maybe, the awful fate she was resigning herself to could still be averted. She should have sought Lady Sylvia's help before, she chided herself. Her pride, and her fear of confronting the new Lord Pendholm, had almost driven her to choose an ignominious destiny.

"Stop fretting, my dear Mary, and introduce me to your sister, will you?"

Lady Pendholm's gentle voice cut short her musing.

Rose approached, a wary expression on her face. She could hardly believe that such a highborn lady would take it upon herself to search for a runaway maid, an expecting runaway maid at that. She stuck out a belligerent chin at Lady Pendholm.

"What does her Ladyship want with us?
~~~~~

Lady Pendholm looked at the fiercely protective, small, wiry woman and smiled.

"I want to atone, Rose. My son Michael, God forgive him, was a wicked and cruel man, who caused untold suffering to many innocent girls. I did not see it in time, maybe I did not want to see, I did not want to acknowledge my son's evil ways. But now, I know. And I do not want Mary, or you because of Mary, to undergo further suffering through no fault of your own. Most of all, I do not want my grand-daughter to suffer. Where is she? How is she?"

Rose was mollified, but undaunted.

"Would you acknowledge the bastard child of a serving maid as a grand-daughter of yours?"

Mary, who stood speechless at her sister's temerity in so addressing a Viscountess, winced at her crude wording.

Lady Pendholm stood tall and straight, commanding and self-assured. Despite her dilapidated attire, nobody could have taken her for a commoner.

"I am acknowledging her now. I know she will not be able to claim her father's name, but I hereby do solemnly swear that I shall do anything in my power to grant her a home, a future and all of the comforts our social standing can provide. And, of course, I will take care that you and your sister lack nothing. Can you trust me, Rose?"

Rose's face crumpled, but still she did not relent.

"And what about you, your Lordship? I assume one of these two blackguards is, in fact, the current Lord Pendholm - am I right?

Charlton bowed.

"I am yours to command, mistress."

Rose looked at him, clearly distrustful of his glib manner.

"Will you acknowledge your brother's by-blow, my lord? Or is she only a minor nuisance to be coldly taken care of to appease your mother's scruples?"

Charlton looked her straight in the eyes.

"Look at me, Rose. I fought for years, for a cause I believed in. I still believe in it, but it would be a void and senseless belief if I did not care for my people, here, in my homeland. I vow I shall do my utmost in the House of Lords to ease the conditions of the poor, but your family is my first responsibility. My brother, through his wickedness, imposed untold suffering upon you all. You are the little girl's aunt, and I am her uncle. You are my family as well, and so do I acknowledge you."

Rose looked at Charlton's serious, upright face and burst into tears.

In the meantime, the little girl, bored with her elders chattering, decided to have a look at the newcomers by herself and tottered on her little legs toward Charlton. She looked at him, made up her mind and held out her arms to him, cooing. Charlton bent and picked her up, burying his face in her curly hair.

"Meet little Sylvie, my Lord..." said Mary, in a soft voice. "You see, I never forgot my Lady. And somewhere, deep in my heart, I knew I would see her again... I named my daughter for her."

Hearing that Mary had named her daughter after her, Lady Pendholm could not help but hug her, crying.

Charlton, moved though he was, thought about Mr Starling waiting in the hansom cab, and thought it better to cut the scene short.

"I hate to interrupt this moving display of feminine sensitivity, but we have a hansom cab waiting for us. Mary, Rose, if you are in agreement, my mother and I have found you a better place to live. So, please, gather what possessions you want to take with you and let's go."

~~~~~

Mary and Rose were stunned.

"A better place? But… we thought… you would help us here…"

Charlton gave a disparaging look at the meticulously tidy, but wretchedly poor little room.

"You cannot live here. It would not be suitable. There is not even a fireplace, not to speak about the windows. Would you not like to have a room of your own? A kitchen? A dining room? A garden where Sylvie could play?"

Mary looked at him with hugely round eyes.

"It is… it is like a dream…"

"But it is real, my dear." Lady Pendholm cut in. "Take heart, gather your things and let us start a new page of your lives."

"Yes, my lady. We shall come. We have very few things worth taking."
~~~~~

~~~~~

Geoff had watched the whole scene with rising admiration for Lady Pendholm.

He found himself somewhat affected by the emotional scene, and comparing the attitudes he saw to those of his own family, *'I wish to God that I had a mother like her,'* he thought.

It was obvious that relationships in Charlton's family were rather different than those in his own, he thought, recalling his own difficult relationship with his brother, and his brother's rather terrible relationship with his wife – his brother's marriage was enough to turn a man off marriage for ever. *'Charlton is a lucky man and I hope he realises it'.*

~~~~~

Once they reached the hansom, Mr Starling greeted them, they all crammed themselves uncomfortably into the cab, and another that Mr Starling had thoughtfully flagged down, and the cabs moved on to Ebury Street, where Mary and Rose would find their new home.

The journey was quite long, and Rose was increasingly worried. They were moving further and further from her workplace - how could she reach it every day, spend her long working hours so far away from home, and get back every night?

Lady Pendholm noticed her concerned expression and spoke softly, so as not to awaken her namesake, who was soundly asleep in her uncle's lap.

"What is it, Rose? Is something worrying you?"

Rose hesitated, but she was beginning to trust Lady Pendholm – really, she had no choice but to trust Lady Pendholm.

"It's the journey, my lady. If we have to travel this far, then it seems that we are going to live very far from the modiste I'm working for. How will I be able to go there each day?"

Lady Pendholm smiled, happy to be able to spring her other surprise.

"Tomorrow, my dear Rose, I shall write to your employer and tell her that I am very sorry to deprive her of a valued worker, but that I have decided to employ you as my personal household seamstress. When she receives a letter on a crested sheet, franked by my son, Viscount Pendholm, I am sure she will not object. What say you?"

Rose burst into tears again and kissed Lady Pendholm's hand.

"Thank you, thank you, my lady. You are an angel, and this is God's own truth."

Lady Sylvia took Rose's hands in hers and did not let them go until the hansom finally stopped.

Chapter Nine

They reached the entryway, as the long receiving line snaked into the brightly lit hall, and Lady Elrington smiled in genuine pleasure and greeted Lady Pendholm warmly.

"I am thrilled that you could come, my dear Lady Pendholm! Such a crush, quite the coup for me, so early in the season. I am sure that there are many here you won't have seen since before your mourning – a wonderful opportunity for Lady Harriet to meet more of the young people."

She smiled at Harriet, who stood, unusually quiet, but obviously bursting with excitement, beside Lady Sylvia. Harriet curtseyed politely.

"And the charming Viscount Pendholm," Lady Elrington turned her warm smile to Charlton, "who, it seems, has begun to captivate the young ladies of the *ton*."

Charlton bowed over his hostess' hand, and rewarded her flattery with his most devastating smile.

"You are too kind, my Lady, I am certain that there are other gentlemen that the young ladies find far more dashing. I am, I fear, rather too prone to plain dressing to attract their attention."

"Fustian! You are a picture of elegance, and far more attractive than those overdecorated young fops. It gives you, if I may say so, a more dangerous air –which many young ladies find quite irresistible. I advise you to take full advantage of that fact!"

With that riposte, Lady Elrington released them, and turned to greet the next of her guests.

Lady Pendholm smiled at both of her children, suddenly overwhelmed with pride in their manner and appearance.

Harriet, close beside Charlton, lent towards him and whispered, "Charlton, were you *flirting* with Lady Elrington?"

Her tones were filled with shock, at the very idea that her brother was capable of such a thing – this was, after all, only her second Ball, ever, and adjusting to seeing her mother and brother in such a different context was somewhat of a challenge.

"Only as much as is polite and expected, silly goose. You will see – everyone indulges in a little flirtation, and witty converse – although, perhaps too often, the wit develops rather a sharp edge, and strays into gossip. It would be dull indeed, if we were all totally bland in our conversation!"

Charlton smiled, and patted Harriet's hand where it rested on his arm, as they made their way slowly around the Ballroom, greeting friends.

They found themselves pausing frequently to introduce Harriet to a multitude of eager young gentlemen of their acquaintance, who had managed to find themselves 'accidentally' nearby. Soon, Lady Harriet's dance card was dangerously close to full, and all thought of her brother had fled, as the excitement of being the centre of a whirlwind of gentlemen, all competing for her attention, swept her away.

As Harriet was escorted to the dance floor by the lucky gentleman who had won first place on her dance card, Charlton settled his mother with two of her friends, and excused himself to go in search of his own friends. He had found himself, from the moment that they arrived, hoping to find Lady Odette in attendance. His eyes had scanned the room, and his attention had been only half on his sister, as he watched the swirl of people, hoping to see one particular dark head.

He was also looking for someone he did not really wish to find. Yet it was necessary that, should the Comte de Vierzon be in attendance, he seek him out and seem interested in his company. He found both Lady Odette and her father, in the same moment. The Comte was bowing to Lady Odette and Lady Farnsworth, who stood on the opposite side of the room, near the doors to the terrace.

As Charlton started towards them, the Comte turned and made his way towards the door leading to the hall, and the card room. If that was where he was going, then arranging an opportunity to converse with him had just become much simpler. Charlton's eyes were drawn back to Lady Odette, a much more pleasing prospect.

He worked his way through the crush of people, avoiding hopeful matchmaking mothers with daughters in tow, and brushing off those acquaintances who tried to engage him in conversation. Some of the *ton* still turned away as he approached, not quite the cut direct, but close, from those, who, perhaps, had families that had been most touched by his brother's terrible deeds. He ignored it, although, inside, he still felt devastated by the damage done to his family's honour.

At least things were improving, and more now greeted them with warmth than turned away. As he moved towards her, Lady Odette looked up, and saw him. Their eyes met, and, suddenly, everything else seemed to fade into an unimportant blur.

He was caught in her intense blue violet gaze, drawn inexorably to her side. Charlton halted before her, and bowed over her hand, his lips lingering a fraction too long for propriety, as they brushed her glove. He barely remembered to greet Lady Farnsworth as well, so focused was he on Lady Odette.

"Good evening my Lord, it is good to see you again." Lady Farnsworth's voice was warm, and her eyes twinkled as she spoke. Charlton suspected that she was quite aware that he had almost been terribly impolite and ignored her. She seemed amused, but it would not do – he could not afford such careless unawareness of his surroundings, when so much potential danger surrounded them. Even if Lady Odette was a most delightful distraction.

How deeply he wished that she was not the daughter of a suspected, nay, confirmed, spy.

"Delighted, my Lady. Both you, and Lady Odette, are looking exquisite this evening, if I may say so." He spoke to both women, but his eyes rested on Lady Odette as he spoke.

"Lady Odette, will you do me the honour of granting me a dance? That is, of course, if your dance card is not already completely full? For surely, my late arrival has given other gentleman the chance to claim every dance. I shall be devastated if that is the case."

His voice was light, but he realised, as he spoke, that he meant every word with an intensity that surprised him. Lady Odette blushed, and finally turned her beautiful eyes down, her shyness taking hold again at his words. Which only made her all the more appealing, because her reactions were genuine, not the false modesty of so many young women. Her voice was soft as she spoke.

"I would be delighted my Lord, contrary to your expectations, I find my dance card rather distinctly empty." She glanced up, and her breath caught at the smile that lit his face. He offered his arm, and they turned toward the floor as the orchestra struck up the next tune.

~~~~~

The heat of his arm under her hand made Odette quite breathless – all her resolutions to not be a giddy schoolgirl about this man were for nought – she found her heart beating harder, and the blush had not faded from her cheeks. She hoped that she did not look hopelessly and embarrassingly red in the face.
~~~~~

Since that dinner party, where she had, so precipitously, risked everything by foolishly quoting literature at him, and he, rather than expressing horror (as she was certain most of the other gentlemen of her acquaintance would have done) had seemed delighted by her knowledge, she had been unable to get Viscount Pendholm out of her thoughts.

Part of her was sure that she must have been mistaken – a gentleman who actually approved of her interest in languages and literature seemed so improbable – perhaps she had dreamed that conversation? Yet here he was, those beautiful eyes sparkling at her, a smile lighting his face, asking her to dance. Perhaps it was actually true? Perhaps here was a man she could be interested in.

Her thoughts fragmented as he swept her into his arms, and she realised that it was a waltz, again. Her pulse raced even harder as his arms held her, and they began to move. She looked up, wondering what she might say, for her aunt had quite forcibly explained that a girl should be able to converse with a gentleman when dancing, to keep his interest engaged.

Her eyes met his. It seemed that everything else, but those deep chocolate eyes with the tiny gold flecks, disappeared. They might as well have been alone on the floor – she was totally unaware of the other dancers. It was like floating, so smoothly did they move together, so skilfully did he guide her around the floor. Any consideration of speech left her. And, fortunately, it appeared that he did not expect it, for he simply smiled at her, his body so close, as they moved, that her blood heated and she felt almost dizzy.

And then, some indeterminate time later, they spun to a halt.

For a moment, as the music ended, neither of them moved, then Odette mentally shook herself, becoming aware of where they were, of the press of people around them, and was suddenly embarrassed. She had not conversed with him at all! What must he think? And they could not just stand here – that would attract attention, and cause gossip – which she most definitely did not desire!

It seemed that Viscount Pendholm recognised this at the same moment she did, and he quickly placed her hand on his arm, and turned her towards the chairs where her aunt waited. Lady Farnsworth's eyes rested on them speculatively as they approached her, and Odette knew that she would be quizzed about her possible interest in Lord Pendholm, later.

Reaching Lady Farnsworth, they stopped, and he bowed over her hand, his lips brushing the back of her glove again, sending a shiver through her instantly.

"Thank you my Lady, that was delightful."

He bowed to Lady Farnsworth as well, then turned and left them, moving across the room through the crush of people as smoothly as he had moved them around the dance floor. Odette watched him go, still feeling as if in a dream, as she sank to the chair beside her aunt.

Lady Farnsworth, however, watched the other young ladies in the room – those who were either following Viscount Pendholm with their eyes, hopefully, or those who were now looking at Odette with what could only be described as envy.

She smiled to herself, and nodded with satisfaction.

Viscount Pendholm disappeared through the door to the hall, most likely towards the card room, and the company of other men. It was as if his disappearing from view broke the spell, and the sounds, sights and smells of the Ballroom crashed back into Odette's awareness like a wave.

~~~~~

Charlton would have far preferred to stay and talk with Lady Odette, to dance with her again, immersed in the scent of her, that subtle blend of exotic spices and roses, although that would have raised far too much scandalous gossip had he done so, than to take the path he was taking. But duty called. He pushed open the door to the card room, where the sound of boisterous discussion met him, from one corner of the room where a group of men, with whisky in hand, were settled around the fireplace. The aromatic scent of fine cigars drifted from their vicinity too.

To the other side of the room, at one of the card tables, the Comte de Vierzon and three others played with a silent intensity. Charlton shuddered, and steeled himself to join them. He never played cards – cards were too entangled in his memories of Michael, and of everything bad that had resulted. Still, if his duty to his country required it, he would play, even if it left him feeling sullied as a result.

He reached the table, and stood to one side, watching. The Comte, as if feeling his presence, glanced up, and nodded, acknowledging him, then went back to his play.
~~~~~

A few minutes later, one of the players, a young Lord known for his ability to lose at almost any game, and his stubbornness in playing regardless, stood, cast his cards down, and left.

The Comte gathered up his winnings and turned to Charlton.

"Do you care to join us, my Lord Pendholm?" There was an undertone to the words, almost as if he was inviting Charlton to join something rather more than a game of cards. Perhaps he was. Time to find out.

"Bien sur, m'sieur le Comte."

Charlton nodded, slid into the empty seat, and waited as the cards were dealt.

Two hours later, Charlton was richer by a small amount, the Comte by a large amount, and the other two players had, with comments about meeting again soon, left them to themselves. Those comments had seemed innocent enough, but Charlton's sense of things pricked at him – it could as easily have been a conversation with deeper meaning, and the meeting referred to one of much greater significance than another Ball or card party.

Taking a glass of brandy each, the Comte and Charlton left the table for other players, and stepped out through the French doors onto the balcony. The air was chill and crisp – it felt good after the close air of the card room, and, for once, the fog of coal smoke from everyone's winter fires had been blown aside by the brisk wind earlier, and the stars shone clear above in the still night air. It made Charlton think of nights in Spain, when the night sky was beautiful, as the darkness hid the ugliness of war below.

They stood, silent for a while, sipping brandy, their breaths fogging in the chill air. Eventually, the Comte looked directly at Charlton, and smiled.   It was not a smile that was at all reassuring.

Charlton waited, wondering if the other man would speak. This was where his skills lay – in putting others at ease, in getting them to trust him, in making them want to speak, to tell him things – things they might not tell others. Eventually, his stillness was rewarded.

"My Lord Pendholm, I have been observing you. And, whilst you are born to the *ton*, I do not think that you are entirely happy amongst them, *n'est ce pas*? They are not kind to you, no matter that you are not your brother. Though you have, perhaps, something of his skill at cards, as I have seen tonight."

The Comte raised his eyebrow, enquiringly, and Charlton forcibly repressed the sickness that rose in him, at any such comparison of himself to Michael. The Comte, seeing no reaction from him, continued, "You have reason to be... displeased with them."

Charlton took his time in replying, knowing that this was a critical moment for his mission. It would not do to agree too easily, yet he must seem sympathetic to the Comte's attitudes.

"They are not all against me. I have some patience – for my sister's sake, if not my own. But yet, perhaps you are right, there are times when it galls me, that I have fought to protect this, yet they treat me with such disdain. Perhaps my sense of what is honourable has been distorted by war. To be treated justly is not such an unreasonable expectation, is it?"

Light flashed off the ruby on the Comte's finger, as he raised his glass to his mouth.

The silence stretched again, broken only by the faint sound of a night watchman making his rounds through the streets below.

"Justice can be difficult to come by, amongst this glittering world of privilege. Yet I agree that it is not unreasonable to expect. I have some expectations of my own. I have sought out, as friends, others who also believe such things. It can be a comfort to be amongst those of like mind."

"Indeed, yet discovering those who are truly of like mind can be difficult....."

Charlton let his words trail off, sipping his brandy, watching the mist of his breath drift in lazy swirls away from him, and waited. It did not take long.

"Perhaps you would find my... friends... of like mind with you too? I will consider introducing you. I am protective of my friends – I treasure our comradeship, and wish it to stay... pure of common intent, if you understand."

At the Comte's words, Charlton swallowed the bitter laughter that wanted to rise in his throat, for such a description could easily be put to his bond with the other Hounds, and to hear his thoughts of that good and positive bond echoed in this tainted context was ironic.

"Truly, *m'sieur le Comte*, I would appreciate such an introduction. I do, quite, understand the value of such comradeship. One can, at times, accomplish something together, which could not be achieved individually..."

Again, the double applicability of his words was bitter in his mouth –that ability to achieve more together than apart was what had made the Hounds so successful – for themselves, and for their country. It was the reason they were all still alive.

He let none of his feelings show on his face. His expression was calm as he waited for the Comte's response.

"Exactly, my Lord Pendholm, exactly. I will consider this, and I will be in touch, should a suitable opportunity arise for an… introduction." He bowed, and it was obvious that the conversation was at an end.

Charlton tossed back the last of his brandy, bowed in return, and made his way back through the card room, to find his mother and sister, and go back to being nothing more than a Viscount with a family scandal to overcome. He felt a little unpleasant, as if the last few hours had left an invisible layer of grime on his skin. He knew it was his duty to do this, but, at that instant, he wished Baron Setford to the deepest hell… again.

Chapter Ten

Now that the Season had begun in earnest, and Harriet was being escorted to Balls and dinners on most evenings, Charlton had fallen into a pattern. His late evenings, even after Balls, still ended with a short coze with his mother in her parlour, where they both discussed the events of the day, the unsuitability of the gentlemen who were pursuing Harriet, his progress with clearing Michael's papers, and also the progress of Mary and her child.

But his day now started with a brisk ride (at a far earlier hour than almost any of the *ton* would ever rise), followed by either more work on Michael's papers, more study of the papers provided by Baron Setford, and the inevitable tasks required to ensure the good management of his estates, or, every few days, a visit to Mary, Rose and little Sylvie. In the afternoons he met with his friends when he could, especially those of the Hounds who were in town, went on the occasional afternoon visit with his mother and Harriet, and generally got on with life.

The evenings, of course, were a continual round of social events – events where he was two people at once – the charming Viscount Pendholm, making the *ton* forget his predecessor, squiring his sister, dancing with Lady Odette when he could, and the spy – conversing with the Comte frequently, and being drawn ever further into his circle of trust.

At some of those social events, he saw others of the Hounds – sometimes Hunter, who seemed not quite himself, and was forever surrounded by the matchmaking mamas hoping to catch a Duke for their daughters, sometimes Geoff – Lord Geoffrey Clarence – who seemed to be rather unhappy, perhaps even more so since he had assisted with the rescue of Mary and the child, and was distracting himself, in a rather out of character way, by pursuing those widows known to be open to affairs. Only they had noticed that he was playing cards, and raised an eyebrow. No-one else noticed anything unusual in it.

After evenings with the ton, the days when he visited Mary and Sylvie were a delight. They were so straightforward, so genuine, it was truly refreshing.

<center>~~~~~</center>

As Charlton knocked on the door of the unassuming Ebury Street house that was now Mary's home, he realised that it was now some weeks since they had brought Mary and Rose to live here.

Mr Starling was still searching for the other girls, but was depressingly no closer to finding them, but at least Mary and Sylvie were here.

Dobbs, the footman that he had employed, along with a maid, a nursery maid, a cook and a housekeeper, to manage the house, and care for the women and his niece, opened the door with a smile.

"Good Morning, my Lord. Miss Rose is working in the sewing room, and Miss Mary is in the parlour with Sylvie. Would you like me to call Miss Rose?"

"No thank you Dobbs – I'll just go through to the parlour. But some coffee would be wonderful, if you would."

"Certainly my Lord, Jenny will bring it up shortly."

As he walked towards the parlour door, Charlton could hear childish laughter, and a smile lit his face at the sound. Quietly, he opened the door, and stood, watching.

There was a scatter of toys on the floor – toys that had once been his and Harriet's, that his mother had produced from an old chest stored in the attics at Pendholm House – and Sylvie was rolling a ball and chasing it. Her little legs were getting stronger, and she could now run, if rather unstably.

With the preternatural awareness of children, she somehow knew he was there, and, abandoning the ball, turned and ran to him, arms raised, asking to be picked up.

He bent down and scooped her up, swinging her high before settling her in his arms. She threw her arms around his neck and hugged him.

"Good morning, my Lord. How is…. OH…. Sylvie… no!   You mustn't pull at your uncle's cravat! I am so sorry – she just loves unfolding any folded material."

"Don't worry Mary – I really don't mind. My valet will be cross with me, but he will cope." Charlton grinned as clever little fingers began to undo the cravat that Phelps had spent almost an hour making into a work of art. "It's good to see her so active and happy – and at last you are all beginning to look less starved!"

"All thanks to you, and Lady Pendholm. I am so grateful! I was so afraid that we would die this winter, when the coal ran out, and then you appeared at my door. I am so sorry that I took so long to trust you – can you forgive me?"

"Of course – I knew that it would be difficult, and I am glad that you can now believe that I am nothing like my brother – I wish that some of the *ton* were as willing to believe it! But you were right to doubt, and to challenge us – although the big surprise was your sister – standing up to me like a little dragon, defending you!"

Mary laughed, remembering that day, just as Rose walked into the room.

"So I'm a dragon am I?   Well… I suppose that's not such a bad thing to be."

She smiled at Charlton, and reached to take Sylvie from his arms, gently untangling her from the wreck of his cravat. Rose hugged her for a few minutes, then put her back with her toys on the floor. Greetings over, Sylvie went happily back to playing, ignoring the adults speaking above her.

They talked for an hour, of what Sylvie had done, what new things she had learnt, and of what was needed for the house, and for its inhabitants. It was taking some time for Mary and Rose to believe that they could have whatever clothes, food toys, books and other things they wanted. They had lived with nothing for so long, that adapting was challenging. Each day, they woke, expecting to find that it had all been a dream, and were shocked anew that it was real.

Sylvie, on the other hand, took everything as her due.

With the delightful innocence of children, she simply accepted without question.

Charlton told Rose that his mother wished her attendance at Pendholm House that afternoon, for Harriet had managed to tear flounces on a number of her dresses, and repairs were urgently needed.

Mostly, apart from fittings and repairs, Rose worked on the Ladies' dresses here, and then brought the finished work to Pendholm House. Charlton assured her that he would send a carriage for her – no need to be out in the cold any more than necessary.

Yet again, Rose had a sense of unreality about her life. No need to scrimp, no need to pay for most things herself – it was all just provided. And she got to work for ladies that she loved (yes, even Harriet's tantrums) rather than for a modiste determined to work her fingers to the bone.

She still struggled with the fact that she had staff who took care of *her*…. it was beyond anything she'd ever dreamed of having.

After Charlton had spoken to the staff, and ensured that anything needed was being arranged, he bid them all farewell and, collecting his hat and cane from Dobbs, who had also done a remarkable job of restoring his cravat to some semblance of respectability, he stepped out the front door, full of the positive feelings that a visit always created.

He was beginning to understand why some men wanted to marry, and have children of their own. If his children, and he realised then, with a shock, that he actually *wanted* children, were anything like Sylvie, it would be a pleasure, not just a dynastic requirement, to have them.

The thought that Sylvie might have died, had they not found Mary in time, horrified him.

~~~~~

Jean-Baptiste Marmont, Comte de Vierzon, rose from his chair and paced about the room. The parlour in which he and his 'companions of justice' met was very ordinary – nothing distinctive, neither old and worn or new.

It was in a very ordinary house, in a very ordinary area of London, on the boundary between fashionable and not quite respectable. Not a location in which he ever expected to see any of the *ton*, except those here in this room, by his invitation.

His plans were proceeding well – he had gathered a seemingly ill matched collection of men, whose sole point in common was their anger with the aristocracy, and their aim to see them overthrown or harmed in some way.
~~~~~

They each had a burning desire for 'justice' – which is to say, for getting what they felt was their due, in recompense for one perceived slight or another.

He did not care if their causes were truly just, so long as their passion for action could be directed to achieve his aims. They met, in this house, once a week, to plan, to discuss who else they could recruit, and, unknown to all but the Comte, so that he could ensure that they stayed in a state of fiery anger about the injustices done to them.

They had, until now, been meeting under cover of darkness.

But, with the Season now upon them, they had been forced to move their meeting to late mornings – a time when the *ton* were not likely out and about, and which would not require any of them, especially the Comte, to miss a social engagement. For not attending various Balls and dinners would be noticed. And being noticed was definitely not what they wanted… yet…

They had just concluded a fairly vigorous debate, regarding his wish to bring Charlton Edgeworth, Viscount Pendholm, into their coterie. Many felt that it was too much of a risk, bringing a member of the British aristocracy, at that level, into their plans, but others could see the wisdom – he was a military man, with skills they could use, a man not valued by his own, and snubbed by many of the ton for things his brother had done. He had reason to be disaffected, and to join with them. In the end, it had been agreed to recruit him. Unknown to the others, the Comte would have done so anyway, even if they had not agreed – but it was easier if he let them think they had some control, for now.

Pausing in his pacing, the Comte stared out through the narrow space between the nearly drawn old velvet curtains of the front parlour window, ignoring the rumble of discussion continuing behind him. A movement caught his eye. The faint sound of the front door of the next house closing came to him. Interested, he watched. A man came down the steps and walked up towards the corner, where a small town carriage waited. A man he recognised. A man that they had just been discussing, in this very room.

To an observer, the Comte would have seemed frozen in place, nothing moving, except the reflection of light from his ruby ring, which gave away the slight twitching of his fingers.

Inside, however, his mind was racing. What was Viscount Pendholm doing here? Who lived in that house next door? It had been empty when they first began to meet here. Then someone had moved in – ah, he remembered now – two women and a very small child with some staff. They had seemed innocuous enough, kept to themselves, rarely went out. Even though the two houses had a common wall, they were quiet - he had rarely even heard the sound of the child when he was here. He had assumed, when all of this was reported to him, by his man who maintained this house, that one of the women was some wealthy man's mistress, parked here with a companion and some maids, now that she had borne his child.

Well now... perhaps that assumption was absolutely right. And perhaps he had just found the leverage, he would not be so crude as to describe it as blackmail, which he needed, to ensure the co-operation of the so-charming Viscount Pendholm.

It would appear that the man had managed to get himself a child on some maid, or perhaps even some woman of a higher social standing. And, honourable man that he was, had set her up here. And dutifully visited her. All of which was something not even faintly rumoured of.

Turning, he called the company to order, closed off their discussion, and dismissed them. Once the others were gone, he spoke to the man who lived here as caretaker.

"George, I have a task for you. I want you to watch the house next door. See who comes and goes, and when. See if you can find out a bit about them – nothing too obvious though – don't go talking to their staff, I don't want any risk of them knowing that we are interested."

George nodded.

"Yes Sir. I'll be careful like."

Satisfied, the Comte took his leave, collecting his horse from the small stable in the back yard of the house and riding off down the dirty lane at the back. He had a lot to think about as he rode. That Viscount Pendholm should turn out to have such a nice little scandal hidden away was rather a delightful; surprise. The man had seemed absolutely clean of all disreputable behaviour, until now.

How pleasing. In all but one way. If the man was so inappropriate as to have seduced a maid, or worse, a respectable man's daughter, and got a child on her, he was more of a philanderer than the Comte had suspected. And that made him a man even more unsuitable to pay attention to his daughter.

He could not countenance the man touching Odette now. He must make sure to reveal the sordid details to her, and demand that she not speak to the man again.

Surely she would be so horrified that she would reject him out of hand. Satisfied with his plan, he smiled as he rode back into the more fashionable parts of town.

Chapter Eleven

It was afternoon, and Odette was in her favourite place. She was curled in a large armchair in the Library of her aunt's house, placed just where the best light came in through the window, and with a view over the garden. As always, she was reading. But today, she was trying to learn, as well. She had discovered, in a corner of her aunt's library, a small collection of books in Greek. She had previously not paid much attention, as it was not a language she knew, but something had drawn her back there.

And, after some careful puzzling, she had realised that one of the books was the Iliad, in its original Greek. Excited, she had gathered it up, along with the translated version that she had read so often, and taken them to settle in her chair. She was attempting to learn at least some of the Greek words, by comparing, painstakingly, the two versions.

She had just concluded that the translation must be somewhat 'interpretative' at times, for the correlation between words and sentences seemed rather poor in many places.

Her mind went back to her dinner conversation with Charlton (for she had begun, in her mind to call him by his given name, however forward and inappropriate that might be), and his offer to teach her to read this in Greek. She wished, rather intensely, for his presence at that moment. And, if she were to be honest with herself, she wished it for more than just what he might teach her of the Greek language.

Her mind drifted away from the books, back to the many Balls, dinners, musicales and soirees of the last few weeks. Events where Charlton had been in attendance, assisting his mother with the introduction of his delightful young sister to the *ton*. Odette had become rather fond of Lady Harriet – she found her occasional childishness rather an interesting change from all of the false sophistication displayed by so many of the young Ladies.

But it was Charlton that she looked for, as soon as she arrived at any event, Charlton whom she dreamed of most nights. Charlton, who danced with her at each event, but only once, as was proper, (but usually a waltz if he could arrange it), Charlton who solicitously brought her refreshments, and spoke charmingly to her aunt. Charlton, whose mere presence could make her heart race, her breath come short, and her body feel warm and tingly in the most startling ways.

She sighed, dragging her mind back to the books. There was no use in wool-gathering, in behaving like a lovesick schoolroom miss. She was quite certain that, whilst Charlton liked her, he did not have any stronger feelings for her. For surely, if he did, by now he would have shown some sign? He was everything proper, but he did not act like a man in love, at least to her mind.

If anything, there were times when he seemed rather distracted in her company, which made her worry that she was too boring, too much of a blue stocking to interest a man like him. Charlton seemed to spend some time at each event with her father, which, at first, she had hoped might have some significance, but, if anything, her father had become less and less happy about her spending time with Charlton.

She would see her father frowning at her, as she danced or conversed with Charlton, but he said nothing, and then, later the same evening, he would be talking to Charlton as if they were the best of friends. It made no sense, and things that made no sense niggled at her mind until she solved the conundrum.

She had come to realise that, whatever Charlton's real feelings for her might be, he had, intentionally or otherwise, thoroughly engaged her affections. She had to admit to herself that she had quite fallen in love with him - a fact that she could not admit to anyone else, and could not act on in any way. For, if he thought of her only as a pleasant person to converse with, or dance with, but nothing more, there would be no point in revealing her feelings to him. Mentally chiding herself for becoming maudlin, she dragged herself back to the deciphering of Greek, determined to learn something of it that afternoon.

~~~~~

The Comte had returned to Lady Farnsworth's home in an excellent mood, and partaken of luncheon with more enthusiasm than usual.
~~~~~

Thus fortified, he set out to locate his daughter, and deliver his ultimatum with respect to Viscount Pendholm. He did not like to see Odette upset, and he knew that she would not be happy about this, for she seemed to enjoy the man's company, but he could not countenance a man who kept a mistress like that to touch her.

She should marry someone perfect, who would be dedicated to her happiness. A passing wave of sadness hit him, as he thought of her mother, so long lost to him, but he pushed it aside.

Finding her was not difficult – for the Library was always the best place to look. He pushed the door open, and paused, struck by her beauty, and her resemblance to her mother, at that same age. The afternoon light streaming through the window made her dark hair shine like a raven's wing, and gently gilded the curve of her cheek. It fell on the fine creases in her brow, as she puzzled at something on the page of the book that she studied.

"Daughter..."

She startled as he spoke, so absorbed in the book had she been. He met her blue violet eyes with his own, again reminded of her mother.

"I must speak with you, and, whilst I fear you may not like what I have to say, I must tell you this."

His serious tone appeared to worry Odette, for she frowned, then pushed the expression aside, and presented him with an attentive, if wary, face.

"Yes, papa, what is it that you must tell me?"

"It is about Viscount Pendholm, *cherie*."

For a moment, a flicker of something, which might have been hope, crossed her face, but was quickly gone.

"Yes, papa?"

"I have discovered something about him, *cherie*, something which makes him a most unsuitable man for you to spend time with. This is something which I would not normally discuss with a Lady, but I find that I must, for I would tell you the truth, so that you understand my decision. I forbid you to talk to him, to dance with him, or in any other way spend time with him."

Odette gasped, and broke in before he could continue.

"But why, papa? He has always been the most charming and polite of gentlemen, and I do so enjoy the company of his sister!"

"Oh my dear, I am sorry to have to tell you this, but I have discovered that he has a mistress. And not just a woman with whom he occasionally seeks pleasure, but a woman with whom he has had a child, and who he has established in her own house, with the child, which is very young, and a companion!"

Again Odette gasped, her mind spinning, her first response complete denial of the very idea.

"No man who would so use a woman, and not marry her, is a suitable man to be near you, my daughter. I know that this will be difficult for you, but I demand that you comply with my wishes – for surely, knowing this, he must now seem repugnant to you?"

For a moment Odette sat in silence, as her heart quietly shattered within her breast. The pain was so great that she was not sure she would be able to speak. But her father stood, obviously waiting for an answer, for confirmation of her compliance with his decree. Somehow, she found breath to speak.

"Yes, papa, it shall be as you wish. I find it so hard to believe, but I must trust that you speak the truth, and accept your decision. I know not how I will go on, for it will be most hard to cut off contact with the Lady Harriet – yet I must, if I am to avoid Viscount Pendholm."

Her last words broke on a small, hastily swallowed, sob.

"Trust me, daughter, for I have seen him leaving the woman's house, with my own eyes."

Nodding, satisfied, the Comte left the room.

Odette sat, listening to the echo of his boot heels on the marble floor of the hall, until the closing of the front door signalled that he had left the house. Then, as if the sound had released her, she sprang to her feet, the books falling forgotten to the rich Aubusson carpet, and ran from the room, fighting to hold back the sobs until she reached the sanctuary of her chamber.

~~~~~

Charlton opened the door of the little shop, instantly fascinated by its contents. Books filled ordered shelves from floor to ceiling, with barely room to squeeze between them.
~~~~~

His first thought was of Lady Odette. What books in other languages might he find in here, to engage her lively mind? But his purpose here today was not books, although perhaps he could find the time to browse as well. After.

He squeezed his way to the rear of the shop, and located a tiny man, sitting perched on a stool behind a counter. His smile reached his bright intelligent eyes as he looked up. Charlton smiled back.

"Mr Bigglesworth?"

As the sign above the door had declared this 'Bigglesworth's Books' Charlton felt he had a reasonable chance of being correct. The man nodded.

"That's me. What can I do for you my Lord?"

"I was told to ask for the workshop." Charlton felt a little like a nodcock saying so, for surely, in this crowded shop, there was no room for a workshop, for any room big enough to meet in, for that matter. Mr Bigglesworth's smile broadened.

"Here to have a chat with himself are ye? Well and good now, just follow me."

Easing himself off the stool, he pushed aside a dusty worn curtain that hung behind him, and waved Charlton through. Behind it, a door opened into a narrow corridor, which ran across the back of the building. Pointing into the dimness, Mr Bigglesworth spoke again.

"Just go down there, and up the stairs at the end. Tis the only room upstairs, so ye'll have no trouble finding it." With that, he dropped the curtain back into place, and went back to his counter.

Charlton shrugged, and, after waiting a short while for his eyes to adjust to the darkness of the corridor, he went as directed, climbing the creaking, rickety stairs he discovered at the end of the space. What he found at the top was a surprise.

Opening a door which was quite as worn and rickety as the rest of the building, he stopped, jaw agape at the room revealed. Light flooded in through two big glass windows (glass! here!), which were actually clean, a desk sat under the windows to one side, and a workbench to the other. Opposite the desk, a table with chairs, and two couches with side tables were arranged near a carved and polished fireplace.

Quality carpets, which would not have been out of place in his own study, graced the floor. Seated on one of the couches, Cecil Carlisle, Baron Setford, was watching him with great amusement.

"Sir." Charlton bowed, barely resisting the urge to salute. Baron Sefton's eyes betrayed further amusement as he waved Charlton to a seat.

"Rather a nice room this, isn't it?" Sefton waved his hand about him. "Old Bigglesworth was m'valet once – this shop is his retirement gift from me. He was always so obsessed with the books, kept finding him in the library rather than cleaning m'clothes. So I saw a benefit to both of us when I set him up here."

Charlton nodded his agreement, impressed, yet again, by just how clever Sefton was, in everything he did. As he sipped the perfect coffee that Sefton handed him, he wondered just how much of His Majesty's business had been transacted in this room, over the years.

They sat in silence for a few minutes, savouring the coffee.

Eventually, Sefton spoke again.

"Between what you've discovered, and what we've been digging into, we are close to having the conspirators identified. Most of 'em at least. We know that they meet about once a week, and we think we know when the next meeting will happen. We don't have the location yet, but we're close. I've got some men who swear they've frozen their extremities off, listening under windows to get this information. The important question here, Pendholm, is when you think you'll be invited to join them?"

Charlton felt a great sense of relief at his words – perhaps this would be over soon – the more he came to care for Lady Odette, the less happy he was with spying on her father, no matter what the man had done, or planned to do.

"I'm pleased to note that you have enough faith in my abilities to be asking me when, not if, I'll be invited to join them."

Sefton laughed, and motioned for him to continue.

"I will see the Comte tonight, at yet another Ball. My sister is having such a wonderful season – she's quite the toast of the town – which is a relief, because with her ingenuous and rather cheeky manner, it could have gone either way! But I must confess that I am so far beyond wanting to attend another Ball that, except for your mission, I would have avoided doing so long ago. I expect that soon, after a card game at one of these damnable Balls, he will ask me to join them. The signs are all there."

Sefton smiled, and his eyes lit with the expression that likely presaged mischief. "Ah yes," he spoke softly, "I'd heard you were playing cards – and doing rather well too. Thought you'd sworn off that, after your brother's deeds. Or have you got the taste for it now?"

"Damn you to hell and back! The cards is something you'll pay for, if you ever want me to do anything for you again, once this is over!" The words exploded from Charlton, full of the anger that he had expressed to no-one else, not even his fellow Hounds. "I hate playing – every night I do it, ingratiating myself with de Vierzon, my skin crawls, my gut clenches, and I feel like I'm covered in filth! I will, once this is done, never play again!"

Sefton nodded, pleased.

"Sorry about that m'boy, but I had to be sure. Wouldn't want to lose you down that rabbit hole." His voice was calm and steady, as if Charlton had shown no emotion at all. Watching Charlton's face, he silently gestured, enquiringly, beside him, where a brandy decanter rested, waiting. Charlton shook his head.

"Well then, it seems everything is in alignment. You make sure to get yourself invited to de Vierzon's little party, and let me know when that happens. I'll send you a message as soon as we have a date, time and location confirmed for their next meeting – be sure to let me know if what I send you doesn't agree with what they tell you. Oh, and I think some extra backup would be useful at this point. I believe you have recent contact with Lord Geoffrey? Do recruit him for me. The boy's the best shot, and the best swordsman we've got, so having him on hand will be a damn good idea."

Charlton nodded – he couldn't agree more. If there was going to be any kind of contretemps, there was no-one he'd rather have at his back. And maybe it would be good for Geoff – he hadn't liked, at all, the morose way that Geoff had been looking, nor the way he'd been staying away from the pleasant young ladies, in favour of the jaded widows. A bit of distraction could only be a benefit.

"Indeed, I agree – I'll arrange it. And now, on my way out, I'll even buy some books – we must make my visit here look suitably convincing, after all."

Sefton simply nodded, and poured himself a brandy, his sharp grey eyes watching Charlton as he left.

Mr Bigglesworth was happy to supply Charlton with a rare volume which purported to be a reliable English to Greek dictionary, and some basic Greek language books, similar to those that Charlton had used at Eton. Charlton suspected that he would be buying books here in future, regardless of meetings with Sefton. Well pleased, and imagining Lady Odette's expression when he presented her with the books, he whistled as he left the shop.

Chapter Twelve

Odette locked the door behind her, and flung herself onto her bed, tears pouring down her face, and great sobs racking her body. What her father had told her was terrible, yet perhaps it was the explanation for Charlton's behaviour. If he did have a mistress, with whom he had a child, perhaps that was where his affections were engaged, and he really did only see Odette as a pleasant companion to speak to at dinner parties and dance with at Balls.

Which only made it worse! She had preferred not knowing if he cared for her, to a certainty that he did not. For, no matter how much she told herself that she should be horrified, and flinch from the thought of him, her heart denied her mind, and chose to love him anyway, no matter how much it hurt. For she could no longer deny it in any way. She loved him. It had come upon her slowly, dance by dance, conversation by conversation, as she had come to see herself through his eyes – as someone whose ideas had value, and who could, perhaps, actually be attractive to a gentleman.

She loved him for the little things about him, and for the care he obviously showed to others, for the way in which his mother and sister valued him, because he cared for them. He was not like most men that she had met – perhaps that very difference was what attracted her.

A bitter laugh broke through her sobs – what good was it to realise that she loved him, when she might no longer speak to him or dance with him, when she must push him aside, and allow that he most likely loved another, when she must be a dutiful daughter, and abide by her father's wishes?

Thoughts tumbling hopelessly, Odette cried herself to exhaustion, and fell into a troubled sleep, haunted by dreams where Charlton changed before her eyes, becoming cold and turning away from her.

~~~~~

Odette came down for dinner that evening looking subdued, but with her dignity in place. She would not allow either her father or her aunt to see how distraught his command had made her. Her father would not go back on his word, she was certain, and her aunt would only worry. There was nothing she could do but continue with as much grace as possible.

"You look a little peaked this evening my dear, are you well? Lady Bellmount's Ball this evening will likely be rather a crush – I wouldn't want you to faint away on me!"

Lady Farnsworth's shrewd gaze lingered on Odette's face as she awaited an answer.
~~~~~

"I am quite well, aunt, thank you for your concern. Perhaps a little tired after the last few weeks of busy social engagements. I am looking forward to this evening's Ball, but perhaps we might attend less events over the next week or two?"

Odette did not like to lie – yet how could she tell her aunt that she now dreaded Lady Bellmount's Ball, for surely Charlton would be in attendance. How would she avoid him without offending anyone? Lady Farnsworth watched her a moment more, then nodded.

"If you wish, but remember girl, if we are ever going to find you a husband, you have to be seen. They can't fall for you if you're not there to see!"

Odette had the feeling that her aunt wanted to say more, but was glad when she didn't.

~~~~~

At the ball that evening, Odette managed to greet Charlton politely when her careful avoidance failed, and they crossed paths. She pleaded tiredness and refused his request for a dance. His eyes narrowed, but, polite as ever, he merely bowed over her hand.

"As you wish my Lady. I hope that you will be feeling better shortly."

Odette made certain to refuse the other gentlemen with the same excuse – she wished to give Charlton no reason to examine her refusal more closely.
~~~~~

The fact that he had accepted it so calmly and turned away hurt, even though it was what she had intended. For surely, if he cared for her, he might have enquired further? Berating herself for a fool, she went in search of conversation, forcing aside her shyness and seeking out the quiet group of wallflowers in the corner. Surely that was a safe place to hide?

And so it went for the next week. They attended less events, and, at those they did attend, Odette carefully avoided Charlton, and was quieter than she had ever been. At every ball, her heart broke all over again. It hurt to watch him dance with others, to watch them smiling up at him as he held them close and waltzed. She held it inside, then cried herself to sleep at night.

Her father seemed pleased with her, when he noticed her at all. He was rarely in the house, and, at balls, always in the card room for the majority of the night. He spent long hours talking with his friends, and it seemed, to her observation, that Charlton was now counted amongst those. Odette found that to be particularly unfair. Why should it be that a man suitable to be her father's friend, could be, at one and the same time, a 'terrible philanderer, unfit to associate with his daughter'?

That week was, almost, the most miserable time of her life, only barely less so than the months surrounding her mother's illness and death. It was as if there were two voices in her head, arguing, night and day.

One congratulated her on her cleverness in obeying her father without having to give Charlton the cut direct, and on avoiding making a fool of herself by declaring her feelings to a man who loved another.

The other continuously questioned her. Did she really believe what her father had told her about Charlton? Did he really have a mistress with a child? It seemed so unlikely, so out of character for the man that she thought she had come to know. Surely, the man who cared so much for his sister and mother, was so charming to everyone, had worked so hard to regain his family's acceptance by the *ton*, after his brother's scandalous death, was not the sort of man who would get a woman with child, then tuck her away in secret? Surely, if he loved such a woman, he would marry her, no matter her station in life?

But... if she listened to that second voice, if she chose to believe that it was not true, then her father had lied to her. Why would he do that? Why would he say that he had seen Charlton, with his own eyes, leave his mistress' house? She did not wish to believe that her father would lie to her....

The turmoil in her mind was exhausting, and robbed her of more sleep – soon, she did not have to lie when she said that she was tired. The thought that she might never know if it was true or not, that she might spend the rest of her life not knowing, was intolerable. What would she do, if she were forced to watch, from afar, as Charlton chose and married one of the fluttering flock of young Ladies of the *ton*? How many times might a heart break, and still hurt this much?

~~~~~

Charlton had arrived at Lady Bellmount's Ball full of anticipation. As usual, the first thing he did on entering the room was look for Lady Odette. Her father was obvious, but she was not.
~~~~~

Tamping down his disappointment, he made the rounds of the room, greeting friends, and still looking for her, all the while watching her father's activity. When the Comte went in the direction of the card room, Charlton breathed a sigh of relief. He would find the man there, later.

Finally, he discovered Lady Odette, near a cluster of young ladies who were not her usual social circle, behind a collection of potted palms in a corner. If he didn't know better, he would think that she was hiding.

Smiling, he approached her, bowed over her hand, and requested a dance, confidently expecting her usual pleased, if diffident, acceptance.

He was shocked when she denied him, pleading tiredness, and rapidly turned away. Stunned, and, truth to tell, rather hurt, he shook himself out of his surprise, and took himself off to the card room. Perhaps it was for the best – he was, after all, trying to trap her father, and prove his treasonous intent. An association with the man's daughter was doomed from the start. Yet he had been unable to stay away.

The sad look in her blue violet eyes, just as she had turned away, haunted his thoughts as he sought the unappealing company of her father.

~~~~~

Lady Farnsworth observed Odette with growing concern. Something was most obviously wrong – she just didn't know, yet, what it was.
~~~~~

She did know that Odette had gone, seemingly overnight, from a young woman who was enjoying herself as she blossomed from her initial shyness, and became used to the attention of gentlemen, to a withdrawn and worn looking girl, with shadows under her eyes, and a haunted look. A girl who now avoided the one man that she had previously shown any interest in.

Anna Trubridge, Viscountess Farnsworth, was not a woman to let someone she cared about suffer. Nor was she prone to letting go of a puzzle until she had solved it. She had not wanted to push Odette – surely the girl would tell her what troubled her, soon. But she was beginning to wonder how long 'soon', might be.

The morning sun glinted off the gold edging on the delicate teacup, as she raised it to her mouth, and the slight warmth of the sunlight streaming through the window of her private sitting room was welcome. Anna loved these quiet moments – too early for most of her friends to ever consider it a polite time to visit, earlier than her niece usually arose, and a time when her brother-in-law had, at least of late, already left the house to go about his business, whatever that was. No-one disturbed her, and she could sit and think, or read, or embroider, as she wished.

Breaking that treasured quiet, a tentative knock sounded on the door. Surprised, she placed the cup on the side table, and bid whoever it was to enter.

"Good morning Aunt, I hope that I am not disturbing you too early?" Odette's voice shook a little as she spoke.

"My darling girl, I always have time for you. But you seem troubled – what is it?"

"Oh Aunt…."

Odette's voice shook more, and she choked back a little sob.

Lady Farnsworth drew her down to sit beside her, and simply waited.

"I… I… I am so confused! I must know what the truth is! It is more than I can bear." A trickle of tears rolled down Odette's cheek, and her aunt simply handed her a delicate embroidered handkerchief and nodded. Odette gulped, and continued, the words pouring from her, now that she had begun.

"I do not know what to believe, for surely my father would not lie to me, yet surely Charlton… Viscount Pendholm… would not… could not… be… as my father has said he is!"

Eventually the confused tumble of explanation had delivered the whole story to Anna's ears, and, apart from internally cursing her brother-in-law for a heavy handed fool, she found herself completely in sympathy with her niece.

She could not believe this of Charlton Edgeworth any more than her niece could. She could, however, more easily believe that Jean-Baptiste had lied than his daughter could.

But why would he do so? Especially when he continued to associate with the Viscount?

It was a puzzle – a puzzle that she wanted to solve, not just because she wished to heal her niece's broken heart, but because it intrigued her, far more than the *on dits* of the *ton* gossip mongers ever did.

"Dear girl, if you find yourself to be in love with the Viscount – and I must say that I, at least, am delighted with your choice of man to fall for! – then we must, of a certainty, resolve this puzzle. For I do not find this in character for him at all – nothing I have seen of him suggests that he might do such a thing. I have become quite close with his dear mother, and he is such a support to her, so honourable in all of his dealings, I just cannot countenance that this is true!"

A smile lit Odette's face, for the first time that week.

"Oh, I am so relieved that you consider it so. For I have been quite maddened by my doubts, and unable to sleep for fear that either thing might be true. But… if Charlton did not do this, then that must mean my father has lied… which I do not want to believe of him! But if he truly thought it was truth that he told me, how can that be?"

A considering expression passed over Lady Farnsworth's face, and she stared blankly at the delicate china teacup as she thought.

"I do not know. Yet. But we will find out. I believe that I must call upon Lady Pendholm. She is wise, and has seen much difficulty over the last years, with the scandalous death of her son, the previous Viscount Pendholm – and, although she has not admitted as much, I believe for some time before that, as the man's behaviour is rumoured to have been of the worst sort, before his death. Perhaps, indeed, it led to his death… I am sure that she will be able to clear up this confusion for us, at least as far as validating the truth about the Viscount's behaviour. She may be shocked at this accusation, but she will be quite capable of discussing the topic."

"If… if you are sure that she will not be too shocked… after all, it is a topic not generally regarded as fit for a lady's ears – then I would be most grateful for your assistance in arranging such a visit."

"I trust in her ability to behave like a sensible woman! You know, niece, it occurs to me that there is a significant point in favour of our belief that this cannot be true of the Viscount – at least not true as it has been told to you. Consider – the Viscount has just returned from serving his country, very heroically I am told, in the wars. Before his recent return, but 3 months ago, he had been absent from England for four long years – I am certain of this, for his mother has spoken of how grateful she is for his return, alive, after so long."

She paused, and Odette looked at her, unsure where she was going with this information.

"Don't you see, my darling, if the child is very young, it can't possibly be the Viscount's, for any child born of his association with a woman here, in London, would have to be at least three years old by now. Yet you have been told this child is very young. It is, therefore, quite impossible for it to be his."

Somewhat embarrassed by this discussion of the interactions between a man and a woman that produced children (interactions which her aunt had been at pains to explain to her, however embarrassing the discussion, unlike some mothers and guardians, who left the charges innocent of all understanding), Odette took a moment to comprehend the meaning of her aunt's words. Once she did, relief flooded through her – the child could not be Charlton's! This did not explain the rest, but if lifted a heavy burden from her heart.

Odette flung her arms around her aunt and hugged her, quite startling Anna with this spontaneous expression of joy. Recovering, Anna returned the embrace, glad to see something other than unhappiness on her niece's face for the first time in over a week.

"I will send a letter to dear Lady Sylvia immediately – perhaps I may even call on her today."

~~~~~

Lady Pendholm had been curious when she received the letter from Lady Farnsworth, but had readily agreed to the visit. She had become rather fond of Lady Anna over the last few months, finding her shrewd observations and sharp wit to be refreshing, as her comments, whilst highly amusing, were never tainted with malice.

The visit would enliven her day – for once, she was alone, with no commitments for the afternoon. Harriet was attending a luncheon at a new found friend's house, with Miss Carpenter, now 'promoted' from governess to companion, as her chaperone. Charlton had gone to Tattersall's with some of the Hounds, having promised Harriet a new mount – one better suited to her 'grown up status'.

When Clarick announced Lady Farnsworth, Lady Sylvia rose to take her hands and greet her warmly.

"Dear Anna, do come and take a seat near the fire. Clarick, please have some tea and cakes sent up. Oh – you do like tea? Or would you prefer coffee? "
~~~~~

"Tea would be wonderful, thank you!"

At Lady Anna's words, Lady Sylvia nodded at Clarick, who bowed and closed the door.

"I must apologise for giving you so little warning of my intent to visit – I have been intending to do so for quite some time, but something happened this morning that rather forced my hand."

Upon hearing this interesting pronouncement, Lady Sylvia was certain that the visit would, indeed, enliven her day – although perhaps not in the manner that she had imagined. It all sounded rather mysterious.

"Do not trouble yourself – my afternoon was, for once, quite uncommitted – I am most happy to see you. But tell me, what can I do to assist you – for your words lead me to think that you do, indeed, need my help with something."

Anna sank onto the comfortable couch, sighing with relief at Lady Sylvia's attitude. Truth to tell, she had, despite her confident words to Odette, been a little concerned about how Lady Sylvia might respond. She was about to speak when a maid arrived with the tea, and waited until the girl was gone before beginning.

Lady Sylvia poured the tea, waiting, with interest, for Anna's words. Over the last week or so, she had noticed, at the Balls and events that they attended, that Anna's niece seemed dispirited – when she saw her.

It had been almost as if the girl was avoiding her family. She wondered if this might have anything to do with that.

"I don't quite know how to begin… I fear that what I have to say may shock you, yet I must tell you this, must ask you a most important question. For this matter closely concerns your family."

Lady Sylvia's heart fell, although she did not allow her disquiet to show on her face. Surely there were not more terrible results of Michael's behaviour to be revealed.

"Let me start by telling you that my niece has admitted to me that she has, perhaps foolishly, fallen in love with your son, the Viscount."

"But my dear Anna, that is delightful news! She is a wonderful girl – I am most fond of her, and so is Harriet. But surely that is not what concerns you? There is more, I can tell from your face."

Anna nodded, and, steeling herself for Lady Sylvia's reaction, she went on.

"There is, indeed, more. There is no easy, or polite, way to say this, so I hope that you will forgive me for raising such an improper topic of conversation, but I must. My niece has been told, by someone she trusts, that the Viscount has a mistress…." The shock on Lady Sylvia's face made Anna pause for a moment, before she bravely continued, "…a mistress with whom he has a child. Apparently the woman is supposed to have been set up in a house, with the child, and a companion, in some semi respectable area of London."

Before Anna could speak further, Lady Sylvia, after what appeared to be a moment of thought, burst into laughter. It lit her face up, and it was obvious how beautiful she must have been as a young woman.

Anna was startled – this was certainly not the sort of response that she had expected!

"Neither Odette nor I could quite believe it of him, yet she has been distraught, for if it were true, and his affections were engaged there, then her affection for him would be in vain, for she would wish that the man she loves also loves her. But… my dear Sylvia, please, tell me, what is it about this that makes you laugh so, for surely, that is quite the last reaction that I had expected!"

Lady Sylvia finally quelled her laughter, which had continued, although subdued, through this last part of Anna's speech.

"Oh Anna, I must sincerely apologise. For, when you began, I had the most terrible premonition that you were about to reveal to me yet another infamous act on the part of my deceased son, Michael, the previous Viscount. Instead, it is this – such a relief! For I know exactly what has led to this supposition – and it is not what it seems at all."

Anna waited, somewhat puzzled, but also hopeful. She sipped her tea, as Lady Sylvia, composing herself, continued. "To explain this, Anna, I must tell you a tale, the details of which I must ask you to divulge to no-one else, save your niece, for it brings to light things that my family would rather have forgotten, now that the gossip that came from the scandalous manner of Michael's death has died down."

Lady Farnsworth nodded her agreement to this request, intrigued. It seemed that there was, indeed far more to this than had been obvious.

"Of course, Lady Sylvia, I will hold this in the strictest of confidence."

"You have probably heard at least some of the rumours about Michael's behaviour?" at Lady Anna's nod, she continued. "Most of them are, unfortunately, true. He ruined others at cards – not by cheating, but by being very, very good at what he did. But he did it with malicious intent. And it seems that he had a range of other dealings with less desirable parts of the community, most of which were not honourable in any way. It is those dealings which we suspect may have led to his death. But quite the worst of it, at least from my point of view, was his attitude to women."

Lady Sylvia paused, and took a sip of tea. To speak of this to anyone outside the household was still very difficult, but she would go on – she owed Anna an explanation.

"Michael liked to treat women as toys in the worst kind of way. He seduced them, used them. He liked… liked….." Lady Sylvia took another breath, close to tears, "he liked to hurt them, hurt them badly. He wanted their fear. I am so ashamed that I should have produced a child who became a man like that!"

Anna reached across and took Sylvia's hand, heartsick for her.

"At first I was not aware of it, but then… then maids began to leave, to just disappear. A girl must be desperate to leave, without a character. And finally, when my own ladies maid went, she left me a hidden note. And I knew then that she, and others before her, left because they were with child, and feared to lose their babies if he hit them again."

The tears ran unchecked down Lady Sylvia's face, for until she had found them all, she could not forgive herself for what had happened. Mary and Sylvie were a joy, but… where were the others?

"Shortly after that, Michael was dead. Am I so terrible a person, if I say that I was glad? Yes, glad, that my own son was dead? Because I was glad. He could not hurt anyone, ever again. I began to search. I employed an investigator – I still do, to search for the girls. So far he has found only one of them, my maid, Mary. With Charlton's agreement, I have purchased a house for them. Mary, her sister Rose and baby Sylvie live there now. My grandchild might have died this winter, had we not found them!"

"But Sylvia, that is wonderful - that you have found them!"

"Yes, but it is not enough! I must find the others. Charlton agrees – any child with the blood of our family in its veins should be cared for by us, bastard born or not. Charlton visits them often, to make sure that the staff we have placed there do their work, that the girls and the child are well cared for. He has become fond of young Sylvie – he will make a good father, when he chooses to marry. But he cares for Mary only as if she were a sister – there is nothing more, I assure you. She has taken a long time to trust him – at first she feared that he would be like his brother, but now she knows that is not true."

"You are an amazing woman, Lady Sylvia. Most matriarchs of the *ton* would wish never to see the women seduced by their son, or the children that resulted. They would wish to hide or ignore the family scandal, pretending it never existed. Yet you have the courage to seek these women out and help them! If there is any way that I can help you to find the others, please, do ask me. I longed for children of my own, but, alas, there were none – I take delight in helping other's children if I can."

"Anna – would you, and Lady Odette, care to meet Mary and Sylvie? I want you to be quite sure of the truth of this, to hear it from Mary's own lips. I want no trace of scandal to touch Charlton, and I ask your help in making only the truth known."

"What a wonderful idea! Of course we would be delighted to meet them. Let us arrange a visit for a few days hence. I must admit, I feel so relieved, and I am sure that Odette will also feel so. Perhaps she will cheer up a little. I fear, however, that her father does not entirely approve of her associating with the Viscount, although I don't, truly, understand why, when he seems quite friendly with him, himself. She is a dutiful daughter, so if there is any chance of your son caring for her, there will likely be some hurdles still to be overcome."

Lady Sylvia's eyes sparkled, and her dazzling smile returned.

"I am sure that I can... explore... my son's potential feelings for Lady Odette, and let you know."

After another cup of tea, and an hour's conversation on many other topics, Anna departed, happy with what she had learned, and even happier that she had found, in Lady Sylvia, a dear friend.

Chapter Thirteen

The fireplace in the tiny back room of the squalid inn smoked. Producing smoke was the only thing it was good for – it certainly did not give off much heat. Charlton and Geoffrey sat at the crooked table and sipped the sour ale. The only thing that could be said for the place was that it had a private room, and it wasn't anywhere that a member of the *ton* might see them.

Geoffrey had been hesitant at first about joining Charlton on Setford's mission, but had been convinced, and now seemed glad of the chance to do something constructive. Much to Charlton's frustration, whilst he had spent more painful hours at cards, and in conversation, with de Vierzon, he had not yet been invited to join the Comte's coterie of plotters. But perhaps it was for the best. Setford had asked them to be here, dressed inconspicuously on this day, and they had spent a few boring hours already, awaiting his final message, which would give them the location and precise time at which de Vierzon's meeting was to occur. He prayed that it would be close enough to reach in time, once they knew the location.

Finally, as midday approached, a scruffy, nondescript boy ducked into the room, dropped a note on the table, and ran off. Charlton lifted the paper, which was a bit crumpled, and somewhat worse for wear from its travel in the boy's grasp, and eased the seal open. He read it, and then read it again, praying that his eyes deceived him, but sure they did not.

He groaned, and passed it to Geoffrey, who read it, groaned himself, and met Charlton's eyes.

"The house next door to Mary's." Charlton whispered, knowing, now, why the address of the house had seemed vaguely familiar. "We've barely time to get there. At least the side he's allocated us to watch is Mary's house. But the risk... what if something happens, and we can't protect Mary and the child? Rose won't be there – she'll be at Pendholm House, fitting Harriet for yet more Ball gowns." The anguish in Charlton's voice made it sharper than usual.

Geoffrey nodded and looked at him. "We'll just have to make sure we can protect them. No choice about it. Now, we'd best move, or we'll not be there in time."

Charlton stood, and despite his horror at the situation they were about to go into, he smiled – for, before his eyes, Geoffrey had transformed. Gone was the depressed man who had been doing little but drink and womanise – here was the man he knew, the skilled soldier, the swordsman *par excellence*, whose reflexes were always sharp and whose attention to the world around him never wavered.

The sight gave Charlton hope – hope that, between them, and Sefton's men, they could capture the conspirators, and still protect Mary and the child.

They reached the house with but a quarter of the hour to spare. Dobbs, in the kitchen eating his luncheon, was shocked to see his employer, dressed more like a common labourer, slip quietly in through the servants door, accompanied by a large man he had only seen once before.

"M… My Lord?"

"Quietly Dobbs. I need your co-operation. No questions, just please do what I say – I'll explain later."

Dobbs nodded, completely puzzled, but willing to do as asked.

"Yes Sir!"

"Good man. Now, there are some dangerous men in the house next door. We are helping some others, in His Majesty's service, capture them, before they can do more harm. For now, we just need to watch that house. Where are Mary and Sylvie?"

"Upstairs, my Lord, in the nursery. Miss Sylvie can be stubborn about going to sleep for her nap in the afternoons."

"Good. The longer they stay up there, the better. And you must not, under any circumstances, tell them that we are here. Now, I'm going to tuck myself into the store room here, where I can watch the back of next door out the little window. Please be so good as to show Lord Geoffrey here where he can hide himself in the front servants parlour down here, to watch the front of the house out that window."

Dobbs nodded, beginning to be a little excited by all of this, and waved Geoffrey towards a door at the front of the room.

"This way sir."

Settling into their uncomfortable spots to watch, Charlton and Geoffrey had to trust that Setford had the others in place. With ten minutes to go, Charlton was startled to hear the doorknocker. Who could be calling at such an inopportune time?

Moments later, he heard voices, as Dobbs greeted the newcomers, and ushered them into the hall. Voices that he knew well, he realised with dawning horror. Voices that belonged to his mother, to Lady Odette, and to Lady Farnsworth. What madness was this? Why on earth were they here, and NOW?

He heard the parlour door close, above him, and the sound of Dobbs footsteps as he went up the stairs – to fetch Mary and Sylvie, presumably. He felt a sense of helpless terror, which brought a cold sweat to his brow. So many of the people, that he cared most about in the world, were right here in this house, now, in the path of danger.

For, once Setford's men moved in through both front and back doors of that house next door, who knew what might happen?

~~~~~

In the parlour, oblivious to the danger around them, Lady Farnsworth and Odette looked around them, nervous about what the next few minutes might bring, but also charmed by the scatter of well-loved children's toys in the room, and the plain, but pretty décor. It was clear that this house was appreciated and well maintained.
~~~~~

Lady Pendholm settled into a chair, happy to be here again, and looking forward to seeing Sylvie. She was delighting in having a grandchild to spoil. Moments later, Mary entered the room, with Sylvie, looking a little tousled and sleepy, in her arms. The instant that Sylvie saw Lady Pendholm, she stretched out her arms to her. Lady Sylvia took her and hugged her, before returning her to her mother.

"Good day to you Mary – both you and Sylvie are looking so much better! A few months of good food and warmth make such a difference – every time I see you, you look more beautiful!"

Mary blushed at Lady Sylvia's words, which only served to demonstrate that they were true. Odette was immediately taken with her, feeling that this girl was honest and genuine.

"May I introduce Lady Farnsworth, and her niece, Lady Odette."

Mary dipped them a curtsey, as Lady Sylvia went on, "I am sorry to intrude on your day my dear, but these two Ladies needed to meet you, and to hear your story from your own lips. You see, they have been told, by some annoying scandal monger, that you are Charlton's mistress, and that Sylvie is his child. I wanted them to hear the truth from you."

Mary looked at first shocked, then responded exactly as Lady Sylvia had done – she burst into laughter.

"Oh no, my ladies, it's nothing like that, I assure you. I have the greatest respect for Viscount Pendholm, he's done so much to help us, as has my Lady here. But that's all it is. There's nothing more between us."

Mary watched Odette with interest, as a blush spread across her cheeks.

"My darling Sylvie isn't his child. Her father was his brother – and a nastier man I never met. Sylvie's the only good thing that came of him. Lord Michael trapped me in my little room in the attics one day, and gave me no choice. Said he'd see me dismissed if I said anything, or didn't do as he wished. He used me, and he beat me, and, in the end, I ran away, once I knew I was expecting. I wanted my baby to live."

The simple, unadorned truth, from Mary's own lips, utterly removed any remaining doubt that Odette may have felt. Mary spoke with an edge of defiance, as if thinking they would have expected her to stay, and do as Michael had wished – for many of the aristocracy might have said just that.

When Odette clasped her hands and smiled at her, praising her for her courage in running away, the defiance melted from her, and she returned the smile.

"Even so, for a while there, I thought I had been a fool to run, that we would die, or that I would have to... to give myself to men for money... when the coal ran out, and there was no food left. But Lady Sylvia and Viscount Pendholm came and found us, and brought us here. The Viscount now – he's an honourable man, as different from what his brother was as can be. Some days I still can't believe that we are here, and safe."

At that moment, as if to prove that pronouncement wrong, a loud noise, alarmingly like gunfire, echoed from the street – or was it from the house next door? They all stopped, frozen in shock, and then looked around, bewildered.

When no-one came through either door of the parlour, and there was no further noise, they began to relax – but for a moment only. For suddenly there was a loud pounding above them, and, seconds later, the back parlour door was slammed open, and three men rushed in, flicking the door shut behind them.

Gasps filled the room, for one of the three men was the Comte de Vierzon. His gasp, upon seeing Odette in the room, was loudest of all. He looked, Odette thought, completely unlike himself. His cravat was disordered, his hair was wild, and his eyes were wilder. He clasped a pistol in his hand. Odette took a tentative step towards him, and stopped, unsure.

A footstep sounded in the hall, and the Comte looked around wildly. He seemed to come to a decision.

"Seize them" he commanded, waving in the direction of the women.

The other two men turned and, before the ladies could react, had stepped behind them, one grabbing Mary with one arm and scooping up Sylvie with the other, the second man flinging an arm around the neck of each of the older women, clamping his hold so tightly that they could barely breathe.

Everyone froze – the ladies in terror, Odette in total confusion, the men waiting on the Comte's further order, and the Comte watched the back parlour door, his pistol at the ready, waiting to see if the owner of the footsteps would enter.

~~~~~
~~~~~

The gunfire echoed in the house next door, and Charlton prayed that Sefton's men had them pinned down, with no casualties on their side. Moments later, to his horror, he heard sounds above, then footsteps thundering down the stairs. They must have gone over the roof, from that house, into this one!

He wanted to run, as fast as he could, straight to the parlour. What if they hurt anyone? But he knew that would be foolish, calling on all of his training, and finding this quite the hardest mission of his life, he crept cautiously out of the store room and up the stairs. He heard the parlour door shut, hard, as he went, and cursed. He found Dobbs, unconscious but breathing, in a crumpled heap at the foot of the servants stairs. Leaving him there, he crept towards the back parlour door. As he did, from the corner of his eye, he saw Geoffrey, as carefully as he, creeping towards the front parlour door.

Charlton signalled that he would go in first, and Geoffrey nodded. At that moment, a voice in the parlour, again, familiar, sickeningly so, cried out "Seize them!". Charlton leapt forward, and opened the door, stepping into the room, to find the Comte, with a pistol pointed directly at him.

For Charlton, time seemed to stop. Inexorably, his eyes were drawn to Odette, who stood to one side, the only one of the women not restrained. She stared at her father, then at Charlton, seeming shocked, confused, unable to act. He forced himself to look away – he could not afford a moment of inattention now. His blood boiled as he realised that the lowlife who held his mother and Lady Farnsworth was nigh on choking the life out of them.

Little Sylvie began to wail, and Mary, distraught, tried to move, but the man holding her twisted her hand cruelly, and warned her to stay still 'if she cared about the child'.

The Comte, seeing Charlton look to his daughter first, reached out a hand – "Come Odette, come to your father." His voice sounded odd, but Odette, not knowing what else to do, did as she was bid. The second she was in reach, the Comte grabbed her, and swung her in front of him, pressing his pistol to her side. She gasped in horror, her eyes, despairing, going to Charlton's.

"So, my Lord Viscount, am I to take it from this that you are not, after all, 'like minded' with myself and my 'friends'?" The Comte's voice was hard, and a little wild.

"You are, *m'sieur le Comte*, correct. I must disappoint your hopes in me, for I find that my loyalty to my birth quite overcomes my resentment of the *ton's* treatment of me."

Charlton, as he spoke, was relieved to see the front parlour door ease slowly open, to reveal Geoffrey, a pistol in each hand. Everyone else in the room was facing Charlton, so his appearance was not detected. Keeping his face calm, Charlton continued his conversation with the Comte, relieved to see that he had dropped the pistol away from Odette's side, although he still held her tightly.

"A pity. For now you are an obstacle in my way. For at this moment, my most pressing need is to leave this house. And you, and these delightful ladies, are making that somewhat difficult. I fear I must do something distressing, if I am to escape this place."

The Comte's meaning became immediately clear, as he raised the pistol to point directly at Charlton. Anguish twisted in Charlton's breast – for the man held Odette in front of him – Charlton could not attempt to shoot him, without risk of hurting, or killing Odette. Odette - who he realised, with the alarming clarity that comes in battle, was the woman he loved.

And then everything seemed to happen at once.

Geoffrey, taking precise aim, and employing every ounce of skill he possessed, raised both pistols at once, and sighting with the greatest care he had ever employed in his life, shot both of the men who held the women. Each developed a neat hole at the top of their spine, just where it joined their neck, and crumpled to the ground, their limp hands releasing the women as they fell. Mary grabbed the crying Sylvie, and flung herself behind the couch. Lady Anna and Lady Sylvia, gasping great lungfuls of air, crawled after her.

The Comte, startled, glanced behind him, and realising that his hopes of escape were slipping away, spun back to aim, again, at Charlton. As he began to squeeze the trigger Odette finally came out of her horrified, terrified stupor. All was clear. Her father had become a madman, and was about to shoot the man she loved. She could not permit it. She could not live, if Charlton died.

Odette twisted wildly, dragging herself from her father's grip, and flung herself towards Charlton, attempting to shield him with her body. Charlton caught her, and pushed her behind him – he was no more willing to let her die, than she was willing to allow him to.

The Comte, sneering, regained his balance, and again raised his pistol.

"Well, *ma cherie*, I am disappointed indeed. But, if that is where your loyalties lie, so be it."

The Comte's finger tightened again, then, just as Charlton expected the gun to fire, a strange look came over the Comte's face, and the gun dropped from his fingers. The tip of a sword appeared, in the centre of his breast, and he toppled to the floor, pulling himself free of the sword as he did. Geoffrey stood, holding the now bloodied sword, a look of great sadness on his face.

Into the sudden silence, Odette's scream rang loud, bringing a still dazed looking Dobbs in through the parlour door, to stare in amazement at the scene before him.

Odette flung herself down on the floor beside her father, taking his hand. It felt cold, and unnatural in her grasp.

"Papa?" she whispered.

"Odette, *ma fille*. I do love you, no matter what I said... sorry, so sorry. *Adieu*."

Blood bubbled from his lips with the last words, and a final sigh left him as his life ended.

Chapter Fourteen

Charlton, after a moment of shock, acknowledged Geoffrey's saving his life (yet again) with a bow, and went to Odette.

Gently, he uncurled her fingers from her father's dead hand and gathered her into his arms. He lifted her, and carried her to sit, holding her, on the nearest chair. She looked at him blankly, then, when he gently kissed her brow, she began to sob. Great, heartrending, body shaking sobs, as all of the misery of the last weeks came out of her, along with her shock and grief at her father's passing.

Stroking her gently, he let her cry, taking the handkerchief that someone passed him, and wiping away her tears. Eventually, the sobbing eased, and she looked at him again, her eyes full of sorrow and uncertainty.

"He is gone." Her voice was shaky, a tiny thing in the silence surrounding them. "What will I do now?"

Her blue violet eyes, still sparkling with tears, beseeched him. She was, in that moment, the most beautiful thing he had ever seen.

"Marry me, Odette? Because I love you, utterly. When I thought you might die, I could not bear it. Please, marry me?"

"You love me?" Her voice was filled with wonder. He nodded, and she smiled. "Then yes, my Lord, I will marry you. For I love you, with equal desperation."

The words rang in the silence of the room, somehow a blessing, wiping away the horror of the last few minutes. All stood, considering, watching the lovers before them, before everyone spoke at once, congratulating them.

Leaving Setford's men with the clean-up, everyone departed for Pendholm House.

~~~~~

Lord Geoffrey Clarence sat in Lady Pendholm's parlour, hiding in plain sight. He had seated himself in the chair furthest from the centre of the room, near the window with a view of the garden.

Whilst everyone else was talking, going over the events of the day, explaining everything, in alarming, and possibly exaggerated, detail to Lady Harriet and Rose, who were both wide eyed and awed at the drama that they had missed, he was simply sitting, staring out the window, and thinking.

He had killed again. And now, more so than on the battlefield, it had saddened him. He was torn. He had hoped for no more killing, yet all of his skills were with weaponry and its most effective use.
~~~~~

He had fallen into a deep gloom these past months, seeing no way to resolve the two facts, seeing no practical use for his skills in civilian life, missing feeling useful, yet not wishing to kill.

Today, although it had involved killing, albeit in defence of those he held dear, had shown him a new possibility. For this was civilian life, yet, obviously, there was a battle still to be waged. And Setford, it seemed, was the commander.

Geoffrey resolved to seek Setford out, and discover if there might be a use for his skills, after all. He had never really considered the life of a true spy – he'd left the intelligence gathering to Charlton, the analysis to Hunter, and the planning of missions to Raphael.

On the battlefield, he'd been happy to focus on using whatever weapons they had to best effect. If being useful now meant learning more about spying, so be it. It was far preferable to drifting uselessly from one club to another, drinking with fops and being fawned on by the women who hoped to become his mistress.

Tomorrow. He would seek out Setford tomorrow. It was time to do something.

He turned back to the room, to find himself observed. Obviously, he had not hidden well enough, he thought, with a wry smile. Charlton's sister, Lady Harriet, was watching him. Her green eyes were wide, a small frown creased her brow, and she unconsciously twirled one escaped tendril of her dark gold hair around a finger, as if doing so would help her think. Perhaps it did.

The girl was well on the way to becoming a woman, he could see. She was undoubtedly beautiful, with a body that was ripening into the kind of curves that any man would admire. But Charlton's tales of her tantrums were enough to remind him that, in most ways, she was still a child.

Geoffrey raised an enquiring eyebrow at her. When she blushed, and looked away, he chuckled softly, feeling suddenly less sad.

~~~~~

Lady Harriet was still reeling from the revelations of the past hour. She had always felt rather bad about not really liking her brother Michael. Now, with so much of his terrible deeds revealed to her, she was glad that she had not liked him, glad that he was dead. That might be very unchristian of her, but she simply could not accept what he had done.

When Charlton had come through the door, carrying Lady Odette, and her mother had ushered in Mary, the maid Harriet had not seen for nearly two years, who was carrying a delightful child, Harriet had been overcome with curiosity. When Lady Farnsworth and Lord Geoffrey had followed, she had been desperate to know what this was about. And when her mother had sent for Rose, who flew into the room, all in a state on learning that her sister was here, Harriet had been beside herself to know what it was all about.

And it was even more exciting than she could have imagined! Charlton was to marry Lady Odette! (which was wonderful – for Harriet had becoming passingly fond of Lady Odette)
~~~~~

There had been a great adventure, in which Lady Odette's father had turned out to be the villain (how very sad for her!) and Lord Geoffrey the hero (how dashing he looked!). Mary's child was the result of her nasty brother Michael's attentions, and her mother had rescued Mary, Rose and Sylvie from starving or freezing to death and given them a new home.

Harriet's head spun just taking it all in. It was sad to hear that her mother thought at least two other maids, who had worked in their house, had borne Michael's children, and were still lost to them. She was sure that her mother and Charlton would find them – after all, they had found Mary, surely they could find the others?

They were all talking around her now, about how the death of Lady Odette's father must be presented in a good light, so that no scandal would attach to Lady Odette. It seemed that the decision was to claim that he had been helping His Majesty's men try to capture the treasonous plotters, and had been unfortunately killed in the melee. Lady Harriet frowned – she did not approve of lying, but she could see the point – she did not want the *ton* to shun her sister-in-law to be.

Twirling her hair as she thought about it – a habit that neither her mother nor her governess had been able to break her of – she found herself staring at Lord Geoffrey. He looked like a hero. He was tall and dark haired, a big man, yet he moved so quietly. He appeared to be thinking too. She wondered what about. Then he turned, and those dark grey eyes met hers. It felt like watching a storm over the sea. He raised an eyebrow at her, a slight smile curving the edge of his lips, her stomach turned a somersault within her, and she looked away, blushing.

~~~~~

Just as things had begun to settle, tea had been called for, and Sylvie had finally fallen asleep, curled in a ball on the couch between Mary and Lady Sylvia, there was a tap on the door.

Clarick entered, looking uncertain.

"My Lady, forgive my intrusion, but that Mr Starling is here. You did ask me to tell you if he called, no matter what…."

Lady Sylvia rose, her eyes alight. She looked at Charlton, and spoke, hope in her voice.

"You don't suppose…."

"I do hope so, mother. Clarick, show the man in – I think we all want to hear his report."

Everyone sat in silence, listening as the footsteps approached. It was the kind of silence that seemed as if the room itself held its breath.

Mr Starling looked rather startled, when shown into a room full of people, but pulled himself together well.

"Good afternoon my Lady, my Lord." He bowed, apparently having chosen to simply address his employers, and ignore the rest. "I have, at last, something more to report. I believe I've found them, the other two girls, Sally and Poppy."

A rush of voices, asking, how, where, when, greeted his statement, and he waited, looking a bit overwhelmed, until they quieted and he could go on.
~~~~~

"They are together – they've been sharing a tiny scrap of a room behind a pitiful little second-hand shop owned by an aging relative of Sally's. They've stayed alive by helping with the shop, and taking turns minding the babies. But there's not been much, and winter has been hard on them. The old aunt is close to death, and the shop doesn't have much to sell anymore."

"We must," said Lady Sylvia, "go to them immediately."

The church was hushed, with all eyes turned to the door.

Charlton fidgeted slightly, nervous, yet utterly sure of what he was about to do. And then she was there.

Odette came through the door, escorted by Earnest Trubridge, the current Viscount Farnsworth, a younger brother of her aunt's late husband. As official head of the family, he had graciously agreed to standing in place of the father she no longer had.

She was more beautiful than ever. The gown of blue violet silk, the exact colour of her eyes, was stunning, and particularly so after a year of seeing her dressing in mourning colours. Her eyes met his, and nothing else existed for either of them. Somehow she managed to walk down the aisle, and join him before the minister. Somehow they both managed to speak in all of the right places, say all of the right things, and get to the part where they were declared man and wife.

Once it was all done, they walked out into a shower of rose petals.

Idly, Charlton wondered where on earth Geoffrey had managed to obtain that many rose petals, when it was still winter. It didn't matter. Nothing mattered right then but Odette, standing beside him as his wife.

They were swept down the steps and into their carriage by a crowd of well-wishers, all of whom they would see a little later, at the sumptuous celebration which Lady Farnsworth and Lady Pendholm had taken great delight in planning.

~~~~~

Harriet stood to one side, laughing with Mary, Sally and Poppy, as the three small children ran around, collecting rose petals from the still frozen grass beside the church steps.

They talked about the children, but Harriet's eyes followed Lord Geoffrey – as they always did when he was present.

Frustrating man – he treated her like she was still a child, although, just occasionally, she had caught him looking at her in a way that quite made her feel flushed, a way that she had seen men look at women they desired.

So, she told herself, there was hope, and she was nothing if not stubborn.

It had only been a year. She could persist. At least he had shown no sign of having a *tendre* for anyone else, either. She sighed. He still looked like a hero – he always did to her. Mary thought he was a hero too – she had been there when he had saved them all.
~~~~~

Now that Charlton had bought that house next door to Mary's as well, and there had been a connecting door put between them, Mary, Rose, Sally, Poppy and the three children all lived there. They had employed more staff, for three boisterous children was more than one nursery maid could handle, and everyone was happy. Especially her mother. Lady Pendholm – oh, that should be the Dowager Lady Pendholm now, she thought - was so happy having grandchildren to spoil – Harriet had not seen her this happy since well before her own father had died. When she had lost her husband, the light had gone out of her mother – now it was back.

<p style="text-align:center">~~~~~</p>

Lady Pendholm and Lady Farnsworth dropped, exhausted, to two chairs at the side of the ballroom. The wedding had been wonderful, the celebration a success, and now Charlton and Odette were waltzing together, so obviously in love that it quite lit up the room. But wait, there, beyond them – Harriet was waltzing with Lord Geoffrey Clarence – the little minx, so she had finally persuaded him to at least look at her. Lady Sylvia wasn't sure that she approved – after all, he was considerably older than Harriet, and a rather serious man – still, who knew what might come of it?

The End

(You'll find a taste of book 3, "Being Lady Harriet's Hero" just after the 'About the Author' section in this book!)

About the Author

Arietta Richmond has been a compulsive reader and writer all her life. Whilst her reading has covered an enormous range of topics, history has always fascinated her, and historical novels been amongst her favourite reading.

She has written a wide range of work, from business articles and other non-fiction works (published under a pen name) but fiction has always been a major part of her life. Now, her Regency Historical Romance books are finally being released. The Derbyshire Set is comprised of 10 novels (7 released so far). The 'His Majesty's Hounds' series is comprised of 11 novels, with the fourth having just been released.

She also has a standalone longer novel shortly to be released, and two other series of novels in development.

She lives in Australia, and when not reading or writing, likes to travel, and to see in person the places where history happened.

Be the first to know about it when Arietta's next book is released!

Sign up to Arietta's newsletter at

http://www.ariettarichmond.com

When you do, you will receive a free copy of the <u>subscriber exclusive</u> novella **'A Gift of Love',** a prequel to the Derbyshire Set series, which ends on the day that 'The Earl's Unexpected Bride' begins

This story is not for sale anywhere – it is absolutely exclusive to newsletter subscribers!

Here is your preview of a soon to be released book in the 'His Majesty's Hounds' series by Arietta Richmond

His Majesty's Hounds – Book 4

Sweet and Clean Regency Romance

Being Lady Harriet's Hero

Arietta Richmond

Chapter One

Lord Geoffrey Clarence tapped on the rickety door before opening it carefully. No matter how many times he had been here, the whole place still felt fragile to him – he was a big man, and worried that, if he pushed too hard, the stairs or the doorframe would simply break.

On the other side of the door, the room was warm as the early winter afternoon's sunlight streamed in through the large glass windows. Cecil Carlisle, Baron Setford, waved him to a chair and handed him a cup of coffee, which was, as usual, perfectly prepared, and exactly as he liked it. One day, Geoffrey thought, he would find out how Setford managed that – the miraculous appearance of perfect hot coffee, when there seemed no-one else in evidence, and there had been no exact time for the meeting.

For now, he simply accepted the cup, and sipped with pleasure. This was a place in which he could be totally relaxed, certain that there was no danger – which was a sensation to treasure.

"You've done well these last few months, m'boy. The Prince Regent appreciates still being alive."

Geoffrey raised an eyebrow, a somewhat cynical expression on his face.

"Is that 'appreciates' in a 'here's your reward' way, or in a 'since you're so clever at this, here's your next nasty job' way?"

Setford guffawed and leant back in his chair, his piercing pale grey eyes sparkling. Once the laughter had run its course, his face took on a more serious expression.

"You always were damn sharp – straight to the crux of it. And you're right about it being able to go either way. But in this case, it's actually a bit of both. There's a reward, but there's also another 'nasty job' as you so aptly put it."

He reached over to the table beside him, and produced a folder. From the folder, he withdrew a large sealed document. Sealed with the Prince Regent's seal, if Geoffrey wasn't mistaken. Silently, Setford passed it to Geoffrey.

"That's the reward."

Geoffrey broke the seal carefully. A minute's perusal of the document revealed that he was now the owner of a rather large estate, located not too far from Charlton's country seat, Pendholm Hall. An estate called, apparently, Witherwood Chase. He wondered what it was like. Gifts from Prinny had an alarming potential to come with 'issues'. Who knew if the estate had been well maintained or not? He may have just been gifted an expensive repair and maintenance bill.

"Do you know anything about it?"

Setford shook his head. "Nothing at all, beyond the fact that it has reverted to the crown after the previous owner proved treasonous. So you may find interesting things within its walls. And that's the 'nasty job' bit. We are not at all sure that we have all of the conspirators in the treason. So, you need to develop a sudden desire to look into your new property – in VERY great detail. I would be personally extremely grateful if you manage to find the papers and other evidence that we believe are hidden there."

Geoffrey grimaced – digging through dusty cellars and trying to find secret compartments in wainscoting might have amused him when he was a boy, but it certainly wasn't exactly appealing now! Still, a decent estate wasn't a gift one received every day. It might even turn out to be a pleasant place. And... far better to spend the next few months, and then the holiday season, in a place of his own, rather than in his miserable brother's house, watching him bicker with his miserable wife. Alfred's opinion of what Geoffrey should do with his life stopped at 'being a good heir and doing everything the way I do'. With Charlton's family nearby, he'd even have good company if he wanted it.

Setford watched him carefully, and smiled wryly as the expressions flowed across Geoffrey's face.

"Yes, I rather thought you'd appreciate having a bolt hole of your own, and a damn good reason to stay there."

"Astute as ever, sir. I just hope it's not quite a crumbling ruin – this 'reward' doesn't happen to come with any convenient cash, to help deal with any repairs needed, does it?"

Setford laughed again.

"A gift from Prinny, that came with money?? Surely you know better!"

Geoffrey sighed, and went back to the excellent coffee.

~~~~~

Lady Harriet Edgeworth arrived in the morning room at Pendholm Hall like a whirlwind (which was not an uncommon occurrence...). Her brother looked up with an amused smile on his face. Charlton Edgeworth, Viscount Pendholm was quite used to his sister's tendency to be all energy – behaving like a good little society miss was challenging for her at the best of times, and here at Pendholm Hall, where they had grown up, she simply didn't try most of the time.

The two dogs lying by the hearth looked up, their sleep disturbed by her arrival, but, after a few thumps of their tails, they settled back to rest.

"Did you have a good ride Harriet?"

"Wonderful! Thank you again for buying Moonbeam for me – she is just the best horse that I have ever had! Poor John can barely keep up with me, and Miss Carpenter quite refuses to ride with me anymore."

Charlton knew that that last statement was the most important to Harriet. His sister's long-suffering companion had never been much of a rider, and Harriet had been making her life miserable by causing her to ride as often as possible during the last year.
~~~~~

"Where did you ride to today?" Lady Pendholm asked her daughter, smiling at her exuberance.

Harriet's face took on an expression which could be described as 'false innocence' if one was to be uncharitable.

"Oh, just across the park to the river near Witherwood Chase." Whilst her tone of voice was casual, the whole effect was spoilt by the blush that coloured Harriet's cheeks. Her mother's eyes sparkled with a mischief that made it quite obvious where Harriet's volatile demeanour came from.

"It's a lovely ride, isn't it? You didn't, perchance, happen to see Lord Geoffrey did you? I wanted to invite him to dinner next week."

Harriet's blush deepened, to a colour that was not exactly flattering against her dark gold hair. Her family teased her about her interest in Lord Geoffrey. They were sure that she would grow out of it. She was equally sure that she would not. It was not a childish infatuation, not at all.

She had decided, when she had first met him, just after he had heroically saved her brother and mother's lives, as well as the lives of four other people, that he was wonderful. He looked like the hero he was.

And he was going to be her hero. No matter how long it took for her to convince him. Whilst she had been the toast of the Season earlier in the year, and had been flattered by the attention of a large number of eligible gentlemen, she had not wanted to marry any of them. She had shuddered at the thought. She knew what she wanted, and she planned to get it.

"He did ride by, in the distance. Unfortunately he didn't see me." She sighed in disappointment, firmly telling herself that he had NOT ignored her, that he simply hadn't seen her. "So you'll have to send a footman over with a message to invite him."

Watching Harriet's eyes light up at the thought of Lord Geoffrey coming to dinner, her mother had a hard time not laughing. But it really wouldn't do to belittle her daughter's *tendre* for the man – that would, of a certainty, only make her more stubborn.

"I will do so this morning."

Harriet produced a large smile at her mother's words, and whirled out of the room again, to change from her riding habit to a gown suitable for luncheon.

....

Read the rest as soon as it's released........

Get

" Being Lady Harriet's Hero"

as soon as it's released – go to
http://www.ariettarichmond.com

and make sure that you are signed up for news and release
notices !

Books in the 'His Majesty's Hounds' Series

Redeeming the Marquess (coming soon)

Healing Lord Barton (coming soon)

Winning the Merchant Earl (coming soon)

Loving the Bitter Baron (coming soon)

Rescuing the Countess (coming soon)

Attracting the Spymaster (coming soon)

Books in 'The Derbyshire Set'

Available at all good book stores and for ebook readers too!

Coming Soon!

Other Books from Dreamstone Publishing

Dreamstone publishes books in a wide variety of categories – here are some of our other bestselling books:-

We have books in many categories, ranging from Erotica and Romance to Kids Books, Books on Writing, Business Books, Photography, Cook Books, Diaries, Coloring books and much more. New books are released each month.

Be the first to know when our next books are coming out

Be first to get all the news – sign up for our newsletter at

http://www.dreamstonepublishing.com